Shenanigans

Gay Men Mess

with Genre

Edited by Paul Magrs

Obverse Books
info@obversebooks.co.uk
www.obversebooks.co.uk
Cover Artwork by Mark Manley
Cover Design by Cody Quijano-Schell
First published February 2013

Contents

3

Introduction

Dear Everyone,

How do you feel about writing a short story for me? I'm about to edit a story anthology for Obverse Books (the press run by my friend Stuart Douglas in Edinburgh.) I'm going to invite a select number of gay men to write stories based in a genre — any genre they like — and maybe more than one at a time. I'm thinking of titling it either 'Shenanigans' or 'Genre Benders.' Then sub-titling 'Gay Men Mess With Genre.' (Maybe 'Gay Men *Fuck* With Genre' would be A Bit Much, do you think?)

I love the idea of writers working in different genres and using the rules for each one... but I do have this theory that when gay men write detectives, space opera, paranormal romance or whatever... there's a bit of subversion and bending of the rules going on. I'm after mash-ups and literary crossovers... a bit of Camp Cosy Crime and some satirical thrillers; sexy confessional tales and some time travel; magical realism and outrageous mythic fantasy.

What do you think..?

So... I'm looking for stories of around 5000 words that

somehow explore that — nicking tropes from genres... or even playing it straight — or zigzagging from one genre to another. A bit of playful experiment, in other words.

It should be great fun, and I'd really like you to be in it.

All best,

Paul

Happiness is a Red Door

Stewart Sheargold

Berlin, 1939

Sophia was crooning her melancholy love song again. Her voice husky with cigarette smoke. Her eyes heavily lidded with kohl. Her long skinny limbs swathed in a red velvet gown, and a dirty fur stole wrapped carefully around her Adam's apple. Her pale shoulders were stark in the white stage light. She sang her love song every night and I knew the chorus intimately by now.

> 'Auf wiedersehen, Auf wiedersehen
> My childhood gone
> My life a heavy stone,
> But when I drop at age's end
> The love I will have known.
> Auf wiedersehen, auf wiedersehen...'

I loved how she lingered on the 'sehen' of 'goodbye', a bittersweet ending to her life and all the wonderful things she had seen. Things I could never know. I smiled – there were things she would never know that I knew now. Sitting here on a bar stool in *The Stork's Nest* I was probably the most insightful young man in the bar. I allowed myself a small thrill of egotism.

Men slow-danced under the blue pall of smoke that drifted under the ceiling. Beautiful youths lounged around the dance floor, eyes darting about the room seductively. Most of them would go home with another man for some little payment. Many of them were soldiers. Some were even rumoured to be Nazi sympathisers.

I gestured at the barman — a burly Aryan youth with a watchful eye — and ordered another gin. I smiled again as I took out the coinage to pay. I was richer than anyone here, even with my meagre savings.

'One for you, too, Dieter.'

'Danke, Herr Stanley,' he said. He splashed the clear liquid into two glasses. I swigged and felt the delicious fire sluice down my throat. Dieter hung about me, orbiting the largest centre of cash in the room. I suppose I should be more careful, throwing such money about. But it was only money, and had never meant anything to me. Money was a necessary evil, but it did not give life or love. And why not flaunt it when I could now? I certainly hadn't been able to before.

'Does Sophia know any other songs, do you think?' I asked, without really expecting an answer.

'Does it matter?' Dieter replied. 'They dance.'

Of course they do, I thought. They slow-dance their melancholy away in a stranger's arms. I knew there would be more than dancing required for what was coming.

'I can sing you another song, if you wish,' said a voice beside me.

A beautiful boy of about twenty was sitting on the stool beside me. His dark hair was parted in the middle and swept back to reveal two glistening green eyes. They gazed at me intently. A smile hesitated at the corner of his lips, a delectable wickedness in him awaiting release. He had high cheekbones and a fierceness about him that could have been frightening if not for the amused twinkle in his eyes. His lips were a dusky pink, the colour of pale tulips.

'How thoughtful,' I replied. 'What kind of song would you sing to me?'

He looked at me carefully, then said, 'I think it would have to be about love. Though it would also be a melancholy one. You have sadness in your eyes.'

I flinched at his quick but expert judgement. His eyes looked into mine with warmth and tenderness, and I realised he was not just flirting with me. He genuinely wanted to know about me. It was an odd feeling. I let my guard down to see what would happen next.

Dieter had left two glasses of gin on the counter and very smoothly left us to tend to other customers. I picked one up and offered it to the beautiful boy with the dark hair and the pale pink lips. He took it.

'I'm Stanley,' I said.

He clinked my glass. 'Eric.'

He smiled, and I lit up like a house with all its lights on.

Sophia had given way to that flashy, filthy entertainer Madame Gussy, who was up on stage in a bright red corset, fishnet stockings and heels, draped ironically with a grey officer's jacket, the epaulettes flashing in the white light. She was singing fast and loose about a captain and his python. Something suggestive that had everyone grinning.

Eric and I danced frenetically around the floor. He was a great dancer, with all the moves. I stumbled through the songs. He kept his hand on my back expertly the whole time, moving me into his rhythm. I laughed and laughed.

Exhausted, we sloped off to get more gin, and then sat in one of the tattered lounges positioned around the dance floor. Eric lit a cigarette and blew great drifting clouds of smoke to conceal us. I knew what happened on these lounges, in the permissibly sleazy outskirts of the bar.

He was talking about how much he liked dancing, and wondering whether he could make a profession out of it. 'What about singing?' I asked.

'I have to tell you something,' he said, and gave me a sheepish look. 'I'm a terrible singer.' He launched into the chorus of *The Lavender Song*.

'We're not afraid to be queer and different
if that means hell — well, hell we'll take the chance
they're all so straight, uptight, upright and rigid
they march in lockstep, we prefer to dance!'

He was right. He was a terrible singer, having a singular drone to his delivery. He laughed when he saw my pained expression.

'Dancing it is, then,' I said.

He kissed me. Those pink lips soft and tender. I felt a wave of emotion flow through me. I hadn't been kissed like that for over ten years. I found myself tearing up. Embarrassed, I broke off and stumbled away to the bathrooms. Down the eerie, blue-lit corridors at the back of the stage. Couples entangled in the half-light. I discovered a free cubicle and locked the door.

I looked at my ridiculously young face in the mirror above the small basin. It was a face I had forgotten. There was a slight impression of lines around the eyes when I smiled, but not a single wrinkle otherwise. But Eric was right – there was an undiminished age in my eyes.

I knew what this place was, what happened here. It seemed I wasn't ready yet, even after ten years. How ridiculous.

There was gentle knock on the door. Eric said, 'Stanley? Are you all right?'

'I'm fine,' I replied around my tears. 'Just a little too much gin.'

I could do this. It was going to happen. I was young and beautiful again. It was 1939. There was dancing. And a boy who liked me beyond that door.

I splashed cold water on my face.

Then my watch beeped. I lifted my jacket and looked at it in horror. It was 8am.

Polperro, Cornwall, 2057

I woke in the bath, in a pool of cold water. For a moment there was such a sense of disappointment that I was breathless. But then reality came thundering in behind my eyelids and consciousness reasserted itself and I was filled up, burdened with the knowledge of myself – who I was, what I had done, and where I was now. I lay back on the cold porcelain, letting the dull ache of another day impress itself into me. Sometimes it required a Herculean effort to get up these days. And certainly at my age.

Somehow I managed to get out of the bath, hauling myself up by the shower curtain. I staggered painfully across to the mirrored basin cupboard and tentatively looked at myself. There was the person I remembered – age-withered, time-encrusted, an old man with white hair and a white beard. And those keen, sad eyes, overflowing with memories and history. How cruel a fantasy to take me out just as I was to start living again. But I knew it wasn't a fantasy. The basin hanging on its pipe, ripped from the wall, the smashed white tiles gathering at its base, they told a different story. And the small red door hidden behind the bathroom wall was quite visible. I had an immediate impulse to pull it open, to go back. But I knew that would be impossible. It only opened at night. 10:15pm. Exactly the time I had discovered it. I would simply have to get through another day. Somehow.

The house was just as I had left it – silent and cold and filled with my half-finished sculptures. Some of them were mere lumps of clay with a perfectly formed arm, or half a head. They had encroached from the small studio at the back and begun to sinisterly populate the house, like an army, silently massing, awaiting an order to attack. I should have junked most of them, started again. But even half-formed they were invested with some personality that I couldn't destroy so easily. I made my way through them, as through an obstacle course where the path is known.

In the kitchen I scrabbled about, found some bread. I picked off the mould and shoved two slices into the toaster. I got the kettle going and waited for its shrill whistle.

A cold white light shone intrusively into the kitchen. I looked out to sea, where the waves crashed restlessly. The village was just visible from the kitchen, to the left. It looked completely lifeless, the fishermen's huts shut up, the town giving its blank, useless face to the blustery wind and the unsympathetic sea. No one came here anymore. God, what had made us move to this silence? The end of the world by the sea.

The kettle screamed. I shut it up. Dragged a tea bag out of a box – the last, damn – and stuffed it in an almost-clean mug. Took pleasure in pouring the boiling water over something so fragile, watching it let out its infusion. The mug steamed.

I knew perfectly well why we had moved here. I wanted to sculpt and paint. I had developed an aptitude for it, had sold some paintings to a gallery in London. I needed space and silence. I needed to remove myself from the fug and the noise and the incessant beat beat beat of the city. It had crept into my head like tinnitus, making me mad. John, a country boy himself, had agreed. He wanted to fish and read and bake and write. It worked for a while. It worked for thirty-two years.

The toast popped. I spread it with blackberry jam. Watched the dark juices spill over the side onto the plate.

I looked at my watch. Christ, not even an hour had gone by. I looked listlessly around the house. There were hundreds of books I could read, there was the television, the radio; there was paint ready to be turned into art, clay to be shaped and moulded into beautiful forms. But I knew that I couldn't start anything now. It would be a hollow placebo until I had the real drug that night. There was no pleasure in waiting. Not after all the waiting I had done. Absurdly, at the end of it all, I had been given my life back. But I had to live it in small pieces. I wondered abruptly who else had been through the door, and why they had hidden it away. Had they realised the futility of happiness beyond the door when you always woke here? But surely the very knowledge of the door behind the wall would itch at you, drive you crazy with unknowable promise. Even so, I wasn't sure I was strong enough to endure the days so I could have the perfect nights.

Perhaps I needed a pet? Something to dote upon other than myself.

I finished my tea and toast. I would take a walk along the beach. Get some fresh air. Air this old, melancholy brain.

I clambered down the old, rotting stairs at the back of the house to the beach. The wind was up and flapping violently in my face. But the sea air, and its fresh, salty tang calmed me. The rushing combers rolled up the beach and exhausted themselves on the sand. How I loved and hated the sea. That unfathomable, chaotic blue, tantalising with mystery. So calm in days of sun, glittering diamonds, luring you in. But I'd never felt comfortable swimming in the sea. I was never in control. John had loved swimming, and to watch him dive in and strike out to sea with broad strokes was a wonderful vision. When he came out dripping, his long, strong legs shining with droplets, his chest puffed out with healthy exertion, how I would brim with desire. I remember looking at him as he rested on the sand, tracing the curves of his arms, his chest, down to his remarkably large thighs. His chest moving in and out as the sun burnished him a delicious brown. I remember looking at him on the cold metal slab, his skin turned blue and pale as the sea. It had lured him in and greedily drowned him – How? How!? – and then spat him back out to be washed up like some old, dead flotsam. I never went swimming again. Even showering makes me uneasy. I guess that was why I chose water when I decided to kill myself. A correlative act to reunite us. Theatrical, yes, but then I'm an artist. Theatre is in my blood.

It wasn't a sudden decision. It had been over ten years since John had died. Ten years I had somehow managed to get through. I had worked through the grief. It still welled up at times, and then it was like a cut that would not stop dripping. I'd be a wreck for days. There were certain songs that set it off that I never played myself, but would happen to hear on the radio – of all of them the worst was Kate Bush's *Wuthering Heights*. It was like a kind of madness when I went into these states. I knew what was happening to me but I couldn't do anything to stop it.

I made it through each day, and then I'd wake up and I'd make it through the next. Painting helped, though I was never very pleased with the murky end results. The action of putting paint to canvas or dirtying my hands with clay, making them chisel out shapes, was therapeutic. I once spent a year making sugar bowls.

I didn't see anyone. Occasionally I'd hear the postman at the end of the lane on his motorbike. I was a recluse. When I was young how I loved that word, had wanted it to define me, had wanted to crawl inside solitude and quiet, had wanted not to speak a single word to another human being for months on end. The reality, as always, turns out to be quite different. My heart was punctured with loneliness. No matter how much art you create, it cannot soothe you, it cannot talk to you, it cannot love you. John loved me. I never loved him enough. There is always one in the relationship who loves more.

Some days I was in absolute wonder at how I made it to the small general store in the village. I would look at the plastic bag in my hand and go through the contents – milk, bread, jam, eggs, tuna, cheese, chocolate, beer – and wonder what on earth I was going to do with those ingredients. Some days I thought I was completely delusional and this was happening to a completely different person. Not me. I was here in my cottage by the sea with my lover, John. John: the swimmer, the fisherman, the writer. The tap-tap-tap of his typewriter keys would keep me awake those nights when he simply had to stay up and write, a bottle of gin on the desk, a cigarette ready to be lit on completion of a chapter. And then – celebration! – he would fold himself into bed, and gently shake me, and kiss me, and we would make love, slowly, so he didn't hurt me. But then I would ask him to hurt me, and he always did. But that was long ago.

Then one day I woke up, and couldn't get out of bed. A numbness had come over me, a great weight, as though something large was sitting on my chest. I lay there for, I realised afterwards, five days. I loved sleeping, that realm where everything is forgotten. I hated waking, that realm where everything is remembered and filled with the excoriating light of existence. After five days I could not ignore the pain in my stomach. I had to get up. But all I wanted was to go back to sleep.

I was washing my face at the basin. The coldness of the water shocked me into a sudden decision. I found two scarfs in the bedroom drawers and tied them together. I looped this long scarf around my throat, lowered my head into the basin and tied the ends off at the pipe. I jerked back, but could not get my head free of the basin. I turned on the cold tap. And waited. The basin slowly filled, the tap gushing harshly. The water was freezing as it touched my nose. My mouth was soon covered, and then my head. Instinct taught me to fight it, and I raised my head. But the scarf did not let me. I couldn't hold my breath for much longer. Bursting, I gave out my air. I breathed back water. And began to drown. The sensation is like nothing you can describe – it is more a realisation of absolute terror, that something so natural to you is suddenly no longer available. An innate survival instinct kicked in — stupid, impulsive idiot! — and I bucked and thrashed and kicked against the pipe. Vision was blackening. Did I really want this watery death? Would John come up from the depths to see me through it?

And then suddenly there was a metallic tearing and a clatter and I was falling backwards onto the cold tiled floor. Gasping in great lungfuls of air I looked up. I had pulled the basin from the wall. The pipe was twisted and water spumed forth from a tear in the metal. Tiles had sheared away from the bathroom wall. Behind them was something red. Slowly, I reached up and turned off the tap.

The hint of that red, the mystery of it – something hidden away – brought me back to life. I demolished the bathroom to get at it, smashing at the tiles with a hammer, showering porcelain across the floor. When it was revealed, I found a small red door, flush with the wall. It was night. 10.15pm. I opened it. I found myself in Berlin, in 1939, in a cabaret nightclub called *The Stork's Nest*. I found I was young again, twenty at most. And then I cried and cried – a hollow, echoing space inside me filling with tears. Dieter found me in the bathroom. He took pity on me. He gave me his handkerchief and poured me a gin.

Berlin, 1939

Greta was dancing her crazy peacock dance, her cocked plumage alert, with eyes all staring at the audience. Her own too-heavily made-up eyes sparkled intensely, wide, darting, fixing for a boy to court. The organ music whirled about her, driving her into leg-kicking ecstasies. For a newcomer her pecking, strutting routine may have seemed crazy. We were all used to it by now. Anything crazy or different was cherished here. We applauded it.

I took a sip of my gin and gazed fondly about at this smoky, ill-lit den that I had come to love. Boys lounged around the walls, chatting, flirting, smoking. Eyes flashed seductively at one another across the room. Madame Gussy, wrapped in a ridiculously long red feather boa, was going from table to table selling her racy pictures. Sophia was perched on a stool at the bar, dressed in her, or rather his, casual clothes – an expensive cream suit and two-tone brogues, topped off with a trilby. Word was that she was seeing a rich American gentleman.

Eric was crossing the dance floor with new drinks. His smile made me fill with pleasure. He sat down and slid my drink across, raising his so we could toast.

'Prost!'

'Prost.'

There was a small silence as we drank. Eric ran his tongue around the sides of his mouth. He was prevaricating.

'What is it?' I asked gently.

He gave a smile, shook his head at my seeing through him. 'I am glad you came back,' he said.

'I always do.' I reassured him with a pat on the knee.

He considered, then ran on, 'Did you go abroad? Some work, perhaps?'

A frown began. 'No. No work.'

He looked at me like a hurt child. 'You were away so long.' He paused. 'I looked for you.'

I put my glass down, sat up straight. 'Eric, how long was I away for?'

He frowned at the stupidity of the question. His eyes hardened suspiciously. But he said, 'Near a month.'

I shut my eyes wearily.

'Is everything OK, Stanley? It was the longest you have been away. I wish you could tell me where you go. I worry.'

I had not even considered the possibility of time winding out differently in each century. Oh I had known there was a small discrepancy – a day back home might be a few days here. But a whole month in a night? Time, given back to me, seemed now to be running out. How cruel was this gift? Was that why someone had tiled over the door? Had they lived as much as they could, and then been horrified, one day, to come back and find everything they had grown to love gone? But who was I to know what anyone else had seen beyond the door? Indeed, how did I know anyone else had used the door? But then why seal it up?

I opened my eyes. I looked into Eric's large green eyes. I smiled. 'I'm sorry for not telling you. I did leave reluctantly. I'm also sorry I couldn't say goodbye.'

'As always,' he grumbled.

'One day I'll tell you all about it,' I said. 'But tonight, we have the whole night.'

He measured me for a moment and, seeing the truth, he sighed. I brushed his cheek tenderly. He leaned forward and kissed me. Then he sat back and looked at me cagily.

'I was talking to Sophia at the bar. Her fancy man is putting on a party, in his apartment, just off Alexanderplatz.'

'Is he?' I said, smiling. 'What sort of party?'

'For artists, singers, dancers...'

'Ah, dancers,' I said.

Eric nodded. 'She says he knows agents who want extras in musicals.'

I raised an eyebrow at his eagerness. He was awaiting my verdict. 'Then we must certainly go,' I replied.

Sophia's rich gentleman friend was a heavy-jowled, loud American named Hank Hawkins, an unlit cigar clamped between his lips he chewed around when he spoke. He claimed to have been in the military but left after a fortuitous run-in with a Hollywood actress (which one he wouldn't say, though from his short but pointed description I gathered he wanted us to think it was Greta Garbo). He welcomed us into his lavishly decorated apartment with great bonhomie, acknowledging Eric's arm in mine with a smile and a wink. Sophia, who had led us here through shadowy streets, went up to Hank and planted a showy kiss on his cheek. Standing next to him in her cream suit she looked like an American gangster. She took out a long cigarette holder and placed a thin Sobranie in the end. Hank lit it for her, and she puffed smoke ostentatiously.

'Come in, come in. Make yourselves comfortable.' He gestured at a mahogany sideboard. 'Gin? Vodka? Absinthe? We got everything. Help yourself.' He turned away and began to run his large hands over Sophia.

I went to the sideboard and poured Eric and I a gin and tonic. I noted Hank had the good stuff, compared to *The Stork's Nest,* and was suddenly determined to get quite drunk.

We were the first to arrive, but gradually more people – all of them young men – knocked at his door and stepped confidently into the large room. Many of them seemed to have been here before judging by their familiar use of the drinks cabinet.

Eric and I sipped our gins and made small talk. Someone put on a record – Marlene Dietrich's smoky tones oozed seductively around the room. A couple of boys began to dance slowly in the centre of the room. There was an atmosphere of expectation, as though everyone was waiting for a command and the party would truly begin. Hank's eyes glittered mischievously. He clearly enjoyed playing the role of ringmaster to the night's entertainment. I wasn't entirely sure I was going to like what was going to happen.

After we had been suitably oiled with a number of gins, Hank sidled up to us. 'Boys,' he started, and I knew this couldn't be good, 'Soph tells me you want to become dancers.'

'Eric's...interested in dance as a career,' I replied cautiously.

Hank's attention swivelled to Eric. He looked him up and down.

'We heard you know some people in the industry,' Eric said, his tone hopeful.

'I do, I do,' Hank replied. Then he locked eyes with me. 'And what of you?'

'I'm retired,' I said quickly, without thinking.

Both Hank and Eric gave me startled looks. 'Retired, eh?' said Hank. 'Perhaps you could tell me the secret of your success.'

I felt compelled to explain, but stopped myself. A mischievous thought came to mind. I leant forward, causing them both to move into my circle. 'I can see into the future,' I whispered.

For a moment Hank was perturbed, but then he grinned roguishly. 'We must have you put on a performance for us!'

'Perhaps,' I replied.

'Oh come, come. Don't be shy. Everybody wants to know what the future holds these days.'

Eric was looking at me grumpily. I had unconsciously upstaged him.

'Perhaps another night,' I said to Hank. 'You seem to have plans already.'

The American looked about him, noticing all the boys' eyes were on this loud conversation. Expectation glittered in their eyes, as they brought glasses to lips, as they sucked moodily on cigarettes. The chandelier poured its white light down on everyone. The place had a shimmering tenseness about it, pulled tight, ready to snap.

Hank smiled at me, at Eric — 'You must audition,' he said — and then quickly walked away into another room. Sophia followed him and closed the door.

'What was that about the future?' asked Eric.

I waved it away. 'Forget it. I was being difficult.'

'No, you meant it,' Eric replied. He was looking at me intently. I wondered how he could so easily see past my obfuscations. 'There is something you are not telling me.'

I breathed deeply to calm myself. I couldn't tell him. I didn't know how to start. But I was drunk enough that I said, somewhat peevishly, 'Yes, there is something I'm not telling you.'

Fortunately, I was stopped from an explanation by the door opening. Hank stood in the doorway, dressed in the long grey jacket of a Nazi officer. His head was down, face hidden by a cap. There was a collective intake of breath. He slowly raised his head and the tense atmosphere was broken by the leer he gave us all. His lips were bright red with lipstick. He came out into the light and brandished a small whip, flicking it through the air to give out a series of sharp cracks. Sophia appeared behind him in corset, garters and black goose-stepping boots, her nipples showing, and her hair covered by a severe black bob wig.

Hank's eyes travelled around the room. 'I have heard that some of you have been very naughty, that you have been indulging in wicked, filthy acts.' He grinned lewdly. It made him look cartoonish and grotesque. 'Who wants their punishment first?'

His roving gaze stopped on me.

I put down my glass. 'We're leaving,' I said.

Outside, on the grey street wrapped in shadows, Eric and I had a blazing argument.

'What aren't you telling me?'

'Nothing. It's not important.'

'Then I am obviously not important either.'

'That's not what I mean. Stop being childish.'

'Childish! I am not the one who thinks he can see the future.'

'You wouldn't understand!'

'Tell me anyway!'

'Maybe one day.'

'In the future? I do not think we have one.' He walked away.

'Eric!'

I stood in the middle of the street, watching him walk away. I was too old for such youthful dramatics. Yet part of me was thrumming, as though a motor had kicked in and was ready to send me across this turbulent sea. I ran after him.

I found him round the corner, stopped in the street, his back to me. I raced up to him and opened my mouth to speak. Then I realised why he had stopped.

'Oh God.'

There was a body in his path – a young boy, at most ten years old, crumpled in a foetal shape, his head bloody. He had been shot. I felt a weight drop in my stomach, and anger begin to rise in me. We stood there, side by side, looking at the body, dumb with shock.

'Who could have done this?' I asked.

Eric's reply was hard. 'Hitler Jugend.'

After a while I was able to move. I knelt down, reached out to turn the body.

'What are you doing?' said Eric, alarmed.

I gently turned the boy over, wincing at the hole in his head, the dark red streams down his face. His blue eyes were glassy. This was just a shell now, nothing vibrant left. I gingerly searched his jacket pockets, and found what I was looking for. I pulled out his papers, unfolding them for his name.

'Josef Goldman, 14 Rykestrasse, Prenzlauer Berg.'

'He's a long way from home,' said Eric sadly.

I looked at the boy – at Josef – wondering what his last thought was, knowing he hadn't known this was his last night on Earth. I was furious at the mocking performance going on around the corner when the very real result was here in front of me. 'We can't leave him here,' I said.

'What can we do?' asked Eric.

I was astounded by his callousness. 'Tell his parents, tell the police. I don't know, something, anything!'

Eric looked at me in earnest. 'You want to tell his family, if he has one, that their son is dead? You want to carry him across town and leave his body at their door?' He shook his head. 'No. He will be found in the morning. We cannot do anything to make this better.' I was about to argue, but he took my hand.

'Come home with me,' he said.

I hesitated.

'Bitte,' he said. *Please.*

And because I was weak, and knowing what he said was true, I replaced Josef's papers, and let Eric lead me away.

We carefully tiptoed through his sleeping family, mattresses squashed together in the single room. In the grimy bathroom of his tenement block Eric slowly undressed me. His eyes lit up at my nakedness. Then he sloughed his own clothes hurriedly. I was so out of touch I wasn't sure what to do next. It must

29

have shown on my face. He smiled gently and came in for a kiss. Those lips, so pink and tender as the throat of a flower. I brimmed with desire for him.

'Turn around,' he said.

I had not felt another's skin next to mine for so long. There was a familiar pain, and then a pleasure I had forgotten existed. In the midst of my ecstasy I suddenly wondered whether he could love the rough, wrinkled man inside the young body. He kissed me and everything was obliterated.

Afterwards he apologised.

'What on earth for?'

'The bathroom,' he explained.

But it's appropriate, I thought, and just smiled.

We laid towels across the cold tiles. He curled around me. 'Gute nacht, mein liebchen.' He was soon asleep.

'Good night,' I said. But I knew when I closed my eyes that I would not wake up with my lover's arms around me. I lay awake, waiting for the future to appear with its terrible alarm.

Polperro, Cornwall, 2057

History isn't all roses, I thought.

I stared out the kitchen window at the rolling sea, and ate another spoonful of baked beans. I ate perfunctorily; it was necessary to keep me alive. Every time I woke here, I was assailed by an overwhelming depression. For all the time I had wasted, for all the things I could still do.

Eric was on my mind. Had he woken yet? I knew the look of disappointment he would pull. And how much time would have elapsed for him in the fourteen hours I had to get through? But worse than that, I was beginning to understand the danger inherent in the darkened streets of Berlin. The danger creeping out and asserting itself. The danger that would soon become oppressive. Josef had reminded me of the wave of death that was coming to submerge Germany.

And yet did I really think it was any worse than the purgatory I was in here, wasting away at the end of the world, the sea's sly coaxing always in my ears? In truth, I had died in that basin. I had been given a red door – pass through, pass through – and it had peeled the layers of age from me and opened up a whole new life. A life of pieces. Jigsawed together.

But as I sat there, desultorily eating baked beans and watching the unstoppable waves crash ashore, I had a sudden idea. It was borne of frustration and was undeniably crazy, but the smallest possibility that it could work made me consider it seriously. And if it didn't work? Well, it would certainly provide me with some closure. Putting aside the cold baked beans, I got to work.

First of all, I would have to arm myself. I went in search of the set of *Encyclopaedia Britannica* I had inherited from my parents. They were boxed up in a guest bedroom that had lately become a storeroom for various things I had lost interest in. It would have been much easier if I still had Internet access, but that was another bill I couldn't pay, and so it had been cut off. I would have to revert to the encyclopaedias. This felt more authentic anyway. I pulled volume A-B and flipped through to the listing for *Berlin*. I pulled out volume W and flipped through to the listing for *World War II*. I began to read.

I took a small duffle bag and packed some everyday clothes into it – nondescript shirts, t-shirts, trousers, and shoes. It took some thought – I didn't want to be deliberately anachronistic. I had decided to take nothing, no token of remembrance. I was doing this properly, without ties, or not at all.

I took the pile of bills on the hall table and spent some minutes ripping them into small pieces. It made me feel much better depriving various rich corporations of cash.

I considered destroying the paintings and the extant sculptures. But, again, I couldn't bring myself to unmake something that held even the smallest semblance of life. In any case, if this worked I would not need to destroy them myself.

The only thing I salvaged from this life, besides the few clothes I had packed, were my house keys. I'm not sure why these seemed to be so worthy of saving. Perhaps they were imbued with the life I planned to leave behind – the first time I put the key in the lock of the small, white cottage by the sea, opened the door, and John and I stepped over the threshold. He had kissed me then, and it connected us, the moment resonating through our history.

I took one last look around at the home I had made and lived in. Cluttered with so much *stuff*. The accumulations of a lifetime. I wasn't sad. This was going to be the past. It had been good. But I was happy to be leaving it now.

It was ten o'clock. The bathroom was cold; a window was open blowing a cool breeze off the sea. I looked at myself in the basin mirror one last time – the slack flesh of old age, the eyes full of melancholy, those damn wrinkles defining me. I would be rid of them. I sat on the edge of the bathtub for those fifteen minutes. I thought of nothing. My mind was clear, as though sluiced through with water, leaving me lucent and pure. I was ready to take on a new persona, a new life.

When my watch hit 10.15pm, I calmly opened the red door and threw my duffle bag inside the small space that was revealed. Then I picked up the tin of gasoline and splashed it about the bathroom until it was empty. The astringent fumes went straight to my head. With some difficulty I crawled into the small space beyond the door. Closing it so there was only an inch open I took out a match from its box and lit it. I let it burn brightly for a second. Then I opened the door and threw it into the bathroom. As I hurriedly closed the door, I felt the heat of the fire bloom as it began its destruction of my old life.

Berlin, 1939

Eric spun me round the dance floor to a whirling jazz number. His hand on my back was steady, keeping me in time, gently coaxing the right steps from me. I looked into his sparkling green eyes and felt sublimely happy for the first time in thirty-two years. Even the dark purpling bruise on his cheek couldn't stop me from thinking him beautiful. I romanticised his injury as a man fighting for the right cause.

It had been three months this time. Eric had been surprised to see me. He'd thought I wasn't coming back. But here I was, suddenly materialising out of a haze of cigarette smoke with a smile, eyes bright, young and vital. Ready to live.

I didn't explain. I merely grabbed his hand and pulled him onto the dance floor. Madame Gussy was on stage dancing filthily, encouraging the lewd atmosphere, encouraging the hip grinding, the leers, the kisses.

I danced with utter abandonment. This was the last night, or it was forever.

Eric could feel my joy and we kissed with gin-fuelled lust.

We danced and danced and danced until our feet were throbbing and we had to sit down. I felt I could do anything. I buzzed with life.

Dieter called last drinks, surprising me. Anxiety flooded through me. I asked Eric to buy us two more gins. I needed their support for the unpredictable morning. I finished mine quickly and then it was closing time.

I dragged Eric out onto the street.

We wandered through the city, dwarfed by its heavy, geometric architecture, until we found ourselves by the banks of the Spree. Our feet hot from dancing and walking we sat down on a free bench. The first tentative rays of light of the new day were appearing. The water slapped and splashed gently, its darkness slowly brightening with the sun.

Eric must have felt my anxiety. We didn't speak. He knew I would explain everything in time. I took his hand and we watched the sun rise over Berlin. The light eked over the grey buildings, splaying them with colour. Heat began to rise into the day. There was a smell of water on stone, and the warmth sent a thrill through my body. Then, abruptly, the sun was clear of the horizon, a glorious burning disc in the sky.

And I realised that my watch was beeping, silently throbbing against my wrist. I surreptitiously switched off the alarm. It was 8am and I was still here. By 815 I was still here. By 830 I knew I was here to stay.

I brimmed with the future. There was so much to look forward to: The Beatles, the Summer of Love, Ginsberg, Warhol, Sylvia Plath, Bauhaus, Bowie, Motown, the Moon landing, Elvis, Hula Hoops, Lego, Hitchcock, Marilyn Monroe, Woodstock, Star Wars. I was breathless with anticipation. I had always felt the past was a better, simpler time, unencumbered by the social alienation of technology. I only had to survive a war. But to die fighting was better than to die alone at the end of the world.

I turned to Eric and said, 'I'm not going to go away again. I'm going to stay here with you.'

He looked at me for a moment, and then seeing I was telling the truth, he smiled. He took my face in his hands and kissed me, and his kiss was like an anchor.

And in the future a house burned, the contents hissing and popping, the wood curling and cracking. The fire burned fiercely, quickly turning everything to ashes. The remains rose into the air and were taken by the night wind, and scattered on the still, cold sea.

Above the Dead Zone
Gene Hult

I truly was not expecting any nookie on Monday evening. It was a Monday! Even if it was Valentine's Day, I was single, and trying to get laid on that chilly holiday smacked of more desperation than I was willing to consciously admit. So my plan was to shelter in my tiny, cozy one-bedroom in SoHo and play *World of Warcraft*. If I focused, I could level my mage up to 58 by solo grinding for a few hours.

But who is safe from the surprise phone call? It was a 212 number I didn't recognize. My agent? An editor? No, it was after 6PM. Who did I know, unrecorded in my cell phone's contacts, who still had a Manhattan landline? I usually let voice mail pick up mystery calls (and most identified ones, too), but loneliness sometimes makes me impulsive.

'Hello!' I answered.

'Hewo,' a strangely-accented voice replied and I knew it was one of the guys I'd flirted with long enough online to give out my digits, never expecting any of them to call, really. I never call. 'I'm Wolf,' he said. *Rolf.* Although his real name was much more familiar, boring, and Biblical. He asked, 'Do you know who I am?'

'Sure I do,' I bluffed. *What the hell is that accent?* He had a silky, even buttery, European voice, with a gentle roll on the consonants. *Beautiful.* I frantically checked the pile beside my computer of drunken notes that I'd scrawled on Post-Its after seemingly promising chats. As I'd feared, there were two notes with the same name in my pile — one cuter than the other, but both potentially having accents. I decided to hope for the best. 'You're the Pisces who's in fashion, who I met on Gaydar.'

'Wight,' he replied. Again, I was riding on the cute accent, like . . . um . . . it wouldn't come to me, the exact flavor of the inflection. It wasn't French, was it? Swedish? I knew Rolf was blond and slender from his shadowy photos. His attractiveness could go either way, as he was 34, only a few years younger than me, and blondes don't always age well. Plus pictures are often deceiving.

'What's up?' I asked. 'How are you?'

'Oh, I am fine,' he said. 'Hanging out. Are you busy?'

I peered at the *World of Warcraft* sign-in screen waiting for me on my computer monitor, and felt a pang of disappointment that I wouldn't be playing. The immersive alternate reality of that game was addictive. But I chose to march out into a rainy February night and most likely have sex with a stranger over the solitary pursuit of killing magical creatures virtually. 'No,' I said. 'Not yet.'

'You could come over,' said Rolf.

'Okay,' I said. 'Sure.' And there it was, the smoky gasp of desire kindling in my solar plexus, the rush of blood to my face, the swelling in my lungs, the sudden flow of the action imperatives of testosterone.

I put on cute briefs, but dressed otherwise in basic jeans, t-shirt, and sweatshirt, utilitarian in February. I was excited, but to make sure my body obeyed my libido, I took a nibble of Viagra. Bundled up in a winter coat and scarf, and carrying a teeny umbrella in my coat pocket, I set off to my appointment in Rolf's apartment.

While he lived close enough for a 20-minute walk, it was drizzling steadily, so despite my umbrella, I caught a cab, mindful of the rain matting down my hair and wetting the cuffs of my jeans in the puddles. I tasted some guilt over the unnecessary expenditure of the cab, but I didn't look good dampened.

On the drive along the glistening streets, I cradled the flicker of desire and the warm bloom of Viagra in my body, and put together what I knew of Rolf from the pieces I'd collected during our one previous late-night exchange of messages. He was a fashion designer, and had an elegantly lazy way of writing, with all lower-case letters and vocabulary chosen with care. He was blond, and potentially very cute, and had that beautifully mysterious accent. He was a Pisces, which meant there would be a good chance that sex with him would be welcoming, encompassing, and emotional. Maybe he would be my new boyfriend. Or maybe I would find him reclined on a fainting sofa in an odalisque pose, a louche, dismissive lad, forever preferring not. But then Rolf had called me.

I got out in an charming area off Hudson St., in the deep West Village. The whole block had the considered neatness of money, with attractive wooden tree boxes along the sidewalk. In his building's narrow hallway, I buzzed up. Almost instantly, he let me in. I skipped the elevator and took the stairs to the second floor — his apartment number started with a 2.

When I stepped out into the hallway, I stopped short, alarmed. The corridor I found had bare concrete floors. In the shrill blue glow of the bare light bulbs hanging from orange plastic cages on the ceiling, I could see that the walls were coated with an ugly, dun primer the color of neglected despair. I strode in, shuddering at the awful atmosphere, haunted with depression and fatigue, maybe even lingering horror. It was like climbing inside a magical passageway carved into a decaying mushroom that led to the home of a hag who revealed tragic secrets. *This hallway would be a classic place to get murdered*, I thought, which made me giggle. There were no numbers on any of the apartment doors. Beyond creepy. I hurried back into the stairwell, and climbed up another floor.

The door on this level was marked with an industrial 2. Beyond it was a bright yellow hall with freshly painted white trim around the doors. It was immediately apparent that this hallway was happily inhabited by the living.

Rolf opened his door as I approached.

'What's up with that second floor?' I asked.

'It's the Dead Zone,' he said with a laugh, backing up into his apartment's dimness. 'It's the upper entrances to the garden duplexes.' His accent was still in mild effect, but he was, I figured, consciously Americanizing it.

He slid into the shadows, but what I saw was adorable, a bull's eye on my type. Floppy blond hair; angular, elfin features, with over-upholstered lips; a compact, slim, muscular body. He was wearing a tight black t-shirt and gray workout shorts and I could see his legs. He had taut thighs striated with muscle, lovely smooth calves, and a long Achilles' tendon, all of which turned me on. I paused for a second to see if insecurity would hit, anticipating as though stuck in the brief moment after you stub your toe but before the pain signal reaches your faraway brain.

Rolf reached around me to shut the door behind me, and lock it, and then he squeezed me in his arms in a quick hug. 'Thanks for coming ower,' he said.

'Thanks for inviting me,' I said. 'Cute place.'

It was dark in his little studio, just the ambient city light through the curtains. His home was chicly minimalist — a bed on a low platform, a simple mid-century modern sofa, a square blue rug. From the short entry hall, I could see large square canvases of graphic portraits on the walls, almost like '80s

Patrick Nagel paintings. I took off my coat and scarf and laid them on a chunky wooden chair by the front door, and then I slipped out of my shoes.

He was lithe, coiled, then relaxed as he sat down on his bed in the darkness, lounged back on his elbows, accentuating his flat stomach. Stunning. 'You're nerwous,' he said.

True, I was indeed nerwous. He was beautiful. And I was not, I knew this objectively. Nobody would call me ugly or even plain, and I can strive for casual cute or handsome in a suit, but never would my face launch a thousand ships, and I'd be lucky if my raw body launched a kayak. It would be easy to imagine Rolf's angular, regular facial features and carved, slender musculature supplying the pretext for a hostile invasion. 'I'm always a *little* nervous,' I explained. 'I vibrate at a pretty high frequency.' That was also true, but I didn't mention, in addition to being shocked by his precise sandy-blond beauty and jittered by my own natural edginess, I also was revving hot on Viagra.

Rolf reached out his hand, pulled me down on the bed with him. I landed on my back, my feet in socks dangling onto the floor, and he rolled on top of me. We shucked our clothing and got right down to it. I was disappointed by this — I wanted more talk first, with at least the appearance of polite civility. I hadn't been particularly horny that night; I had been feeling solitary.

42

Fooling around was comfortable, natural, even though he was so pretty. I kept surprising us both by not being surprised by him, evidenced by his raised eyebrow and mellow chuckle as I slid my hand up his shirt and slipped my fingertip over his tightened nipple; I think we both expected I would treat him like an untouchable China doll, but he seemed to invite contact and I felt welcome to explore. I'd dreamed about touching a body like his: the tight symmetrical planes of his stomach and chest, his unblemished satin skin, the hairless bubblebutt. The dick was nice — he told me defensively it was uncut as I approached it, but I was pleased to see an uncircumcised wang. I will always resent my parents and a sexually repressive society for cutting me in the first place. Rolf had big, wobbly balls, with a good heft in my hand. Under the soft ministrations of my fingertips, I discovered a strange, slick texture to a large patch of his scrotum. In the muted light, I couldn't make out the cause of that slippery section of his sac, but I conjectured that it was the result of some ancient scarring.

Rolf was a good kisser, mostly. The breath was nice, the lips were wonderfully lush and soft, but occasionally he would flap his big tongue rapidly into my mouth, which reminded me of a donkey licking up oats. This should have been more of a turn off than it was.

I was into it. My boner was immediate and raging. It didn't waver in its approval at all, jutting and impressively alert. I was so hard that my pubic area ached. His nipples were even more sensitive than I at first suspected — a tweak made him twitch and moan. So delicious.

Rolf loved giving blow jobs. 'My favorite position,' he said, arranging me in a seated posture on the edge of the bed while he kneeled on the floor between my legs and sucked my cock. Blow jobs were not my favorite — they were too unspecific in sensation — but he was so enthusiastic and sweet that I enjoyed myself. I reached down and ruffled his hair, which was rabbit-soft and a sumptuous Patrician blond texture. The nape of his neck was buzzed high, and I rubbed that silky stubble, moved. I would need to explain my entire life story in order to limn all the intricacies of why that particular Nazi haircut ignited my rocket, so, simply and reductively: I grew up adoring New Wave music in my '80s adolescence, the main drama of my high school love life involved a willowy German exchange student, and I chose Rolf's pseudonym to reference one of my favorite classic movie musicals. *I am seventeen, going on eighteen. I'll . . . take care . . . of you.* Yeah, Rolf in *The Sound of Music* ended up betraying the von Trapps to Hitler, but he had great hair. And a spectacular ass.

'Is okay,' Rolf gasped, 'if I do poppers?'

'Fine with me,' I replied, 'as long as I don't have to do them myself.'

He grinned, ferreted out a bottle from under the bed, and inhaled into a curved knuckle around the bottle's little mouth. I caught the sharp scent and exhaled to avoid it. Rolf smiled again, dopier this time, and resumed blowing me.

Soon enough, I got bored with that. A guy really had to be a certified master cocksucker to keep my dick entertained, as I had very few fellatio fetishes. To me, it didn't signify as erotic as much as kissing, fucking, or even mutual masturbation did — I generally fast-forwarded blow job scenes in porn. So I pulled him up to me and we were kissing again, and yanking each other's cocks. His hand was surprisingly rough, but then perhaps he had to sew and handle fabrics often.

'Do you have any lube?' I asked.

Rolf sat up, stared for a second at his nightstand, and then smiled. 'No, sowy,' he said. 'I don't think.'

Uncircumcised boys often didn't need lube to masturbate, lucky fuckers — but that also didn't bode well for anal sex. No lube often equaled no condoms, and there wasn't any way to use a condom without lube. Spit wasn't going to do it.

'I need *something*,' I said. 'Moisturizer? Even conditioner.'

'Oh,' he said. 'Yes.' He stood up, and stepped over to a full-length mirror. On the floor under the mirror was a sleek toiletries case, which he bent over and unzipped, ass in the air, sideways to me in gorgeous profile. Rolf straightened up and handed me a tiny travel tub of Vaseline jelly. 'Okay?' he asked.

I nodded, opening the tub. It would suffice, sort of, since it was ineffective to use petroleum with a prophylactic, but at least I wouldn't chafe.

Then he was on all fours and I was kneeling between his legs, teasing his hole with my slicked cockhead. Although relaxed and pink, his butthole was not my idol of the anus, frankly. He reached through his legs and tried to hide a hemorrhoid with his finger, as if I couldn't tell. I was intimately familiar with the pain and heartbreak of hemorrhoids — another reason I was such a wretched bottom. But I would go slow and not hurt him.

Rolf moaned from the contact of my dick on his asshole, and dropped his hand. He shifted abruptly and my cockhead slipped inside. I instantly succumbed to the biological imperative to penetrate — I thrusted. And stopped, and pulled out, because I was not a stupid animal.

He flipped onto his back and I leaned over him, balls against balls. Mashing perineums together was a complicated and enthralling sensation, as was grinding into his taint with my rolling pin of a cock shaft.

'You're beautiful,' I told him.

He appeared saddened by this. 'What's your definition of beauty?' he asked.

'You look like a sculpture of David,' I said. 'Not the Michelangelo one. The other one . . . it's a famous bronze . . .' It was skinnier, I wanted to say, but I was unsure if that would offend him.

It really annoyed me that I couldn't think of the sculptor's name. Of course, I now looked it up on the Internet — it was Donatello. He resembled an alabaster version of Donatello's *David*. I wished I could have remembered that to tell him at the time.

Since I knew that Pisceans rule the feet, I raised his left foot and kissed it in the hollow behind the ankle, nuzzling his sexy long heel. I licked the side arch, the bridge with its idealized hump like a cobbler's dummy, while moving up slowly toward his toes. The little toe tasted good — clean and dry — and so I licked all his toes, in the sheltered crevasses between them, and Rolf was trembling in pleasure.

In an organic movement, a blur of adjustment, I raised his legs and leaned forward and my dick was inside him again. I fell onto his chest, pumped deep. Entire lifetimes could be spent examining and considering that subterranean point of connection, the uniqueness of every merger with the physical other, the heat of physical communion.

But I was not wearing a condom. I pulled out and he scooted away from me, onto his pillows. 'Before we get cowied away,' he said.

I was already cowied away. I stared down at him, at the golden expanse of his hairless chest, the sculpted muscles bunching beside his collarbone. 'Hey,' I said. 'Are you negative or positive?' It was a futile question, really, with all the liars in the world. Especially Pisceans.

'Actuawy, I'm negative,' Rolf replied, holding his gaze steady to signify seriousness. 'Just got tested in Nowember. I have the paperwork around here if you want to see.'

'I'm negative, too,' I said, although I had a specter of doubt. It was unlikely that I'd caught any internal STDs during the past few months of being single, but it wasn't impossible. I had had sex. Sometimes rough sex, and there had been at least one short, thoughtless moment of unsafe penetration previously. 'I just broke up with my boyfriend in November,' I said, 'and I was tested while going out with him. . . .'

This was not a sexy conversation, and however necessary, it was a bizarrely intimate chat to be having with a stranger. It was a tremendous leap of faith to believe what you were told, into breathtaking gullibility, and not one that was worth the risk. Men lied like big dogs to initiate sex, fibbed easily during sex to keep it from stopping, and bore serious fucking false witness after sex if we wanted it to happen again.

I flopped down next to Rolf and we jacked each other side by side, kissing. Nice. I turned toward him, slid my knees under one of his legs, and then my dick was in his ass again, going deep.

It felt so appropriate already. *You sick psycho fuck.*

I eased onto my back and he reoriented on top of me, *ride 'em cowboy*! After a few moments of that entertainment, he swiveled around backwards and I held onto his hips as he pistoned the cylinder of his exquisite ass, enjoying the scrape of his ring on my shaft. Then the sensation was wrong. The wrong . . . consistency. There was too much drag, a rasping, muddy texture.

I reached down, and . . . yep, poop. 'Excuse me,' I said, and I rolled out of the bed, heading for the bathroom.

'Sowy,' he called after me in his cute accent, suddenly thicker. 'The smell. . . .'

Rolf's bathroom was modern, immaculate, and gleaming in shockingly crisp lighting, with navy and white tile. Avoiding my reflection in the mirror, I dropped my junk over the edge of the sink's porcelain bowl and warmed up the water while I checked out the situation — not too bad, just a little shit, easily washed off with anti-bacterial hand soap from a dispenser and hot water. My boner did not fade at all. *That's Viagra for you.*

I returned to the bed with a wet crotch, and we kissed and started back up again. It would need to be over soon, though — I could feel myself crashing, needing to be alone again, if only to dwell on the moment I was currently experiencing. I concentrated on jacking him, prodding his perineum, until he came. Then I jerked myself off while he kissed me like he was lapping my orgasm out of my mouth.

After toweling off, we reclined with my head on his chest. My arm was across his shallow stomach. 'Thanks for calling me,' I said.

'Nice Walentine's Day?' he asked.

'Yes, Valentine's Day,' I said. 'I almost forgot.'

We started chatting, highlighting for each other where we were from — me, Manhattan, he born and raised in Europe, that vague conglomerate land. We talked about our families, number of siblings, our jobs; typical post-coital blather. Rolf told me that he couldn't be bothered having sex that often. 'Too much twuble,' he declared. 'But I'm happy I made an exception with you.'

I quickly conjured up images from his daily life, how often he must be hit on, ducking his head in elevators to avoid admiring gazes, laughing off a come-on in the studio's clothes storage closet, how pervasive the intrusion of everyone's attraction. I was consistently surprised by how nice he was, how nice he was being to me. That accent. Was it German? Yes? Italian? Yes? A little British? Just a bit. Swiss?

There were more words without import, just for the tenuous connection of staving off loneliness. I asked him if he wanted me to go home.

'No,' he replied. 'Not necessawily. It's not that late.'

After even more affable chit-chat, we resumed kissing. 'I could come again,' Rolf said, and my boner returned, and he was blowing me. Then I took over my cock, jerking myself off relatively quickly.

'Can I keep on?' he asked. 'To finish?'

'Sure,' I said, feeling magnanimous in the afterglow of a second orgasm.

He slid to the floor, and set himself up again in his favorite position, with me lying on my back and my legs off the side of the bed, while he kneeled between my legs. If he wanted to suck on a flaccid cock in order to get himself off, it certainly didn't bother me. Such was the potency of my attraction for him, my dick never fully deflated in the next half-hour blowing session that it took him to pop.

After coming twice, we were both tired — his eyes became heavy-lidded — and so I started pulling my clothes on. He put on a short-sleeved black polo shirt but no pants and when he turned around I could see that he had a particularly prominent coccyx bone. Odd that I hadn't noticed that when I was fucking him.

As I was tying my shoelaces, I glanced at the photos on the wall near the bed, which were a sequence of small frames featuring Baryshnikov.

'My father knows him,' Rolf supplied. 'My stepfather. I met him once. Baryshnikov. At a party. They were taping an episowde of *Sex in the City*. I also met Sarah Jessica Parker.'

Rolf also revealed that his stepfather was loaded and paid for the little studio in that great neighborhood. I stayed and listened as he talked more about fashion design. We told each other our surnames. He yawned, so I stepped up my exit procedure.

Baryshnikov. *Oh!*

Russian.

As I shrugged into my coat, Rolf asked, 'Do you need any clowthes?'

'Oh, yes, sure,' I said. He was a fashion designer, and everything about him spoke of good taste, stylish and neat. I wasn't an idiot, at least when it came to freebies.

He opened his closet and slid out a sweater with a full-length zipper down its front. It was a wheat-colored cardigan. 'It's cashmere,' he said. 'I designed it.'

'Nice gift,' I said. 'Are you sure?'

'Happy Walentine's day,' Rolf replied. He smirked. 'It's payment.'

I laughed at that, kissed him, and left.

As soon as I was in the elevator, the guilt and self-recrimination kicked in full-force. *You stupid fucking idiot. You suicidal fucker.*

It was pouring outside. *Fuck it,* I thought — I was only twenty-five blocks from my house and I had an umbrella. I walked home through the deserted downtown streets at 1AM in the cold, blustery rain, holding my umbrella before me like a prow to deflect the wind-driven, horizontally-sheeting downpour.

I deserved the cold, wet walk.

Was this whole unsafe episode a way of doing something dangerous to myself now that I'd quit smoking? Did I really just not care that much about my own life, my own future, that I would jeopardize it for a moment's pleasure, bowing down before his beauty? If that was true, what did that mean for the currency of my own self-worth?

I would have to go into denial about my unsafe sex until enough time passed for me to get tested with accurate results. Or maybe I'd order a HIV test kit off the Internet. Apparently, those kits were legal in Europe and could be delivered discreetly.

I was anxious, but halfway home with cold, soaked jean cuffs, the fear of my demise was already slipping away.

I'll be fine.

I jumped over a small stream of rapids swirling down the gutters of Sixth Avenue, crossing over, heading east.

I'm a stupid fucking idiot.

Man, wasn't Rolf so beautiful.

They Sing The Horizon

Matt Cresswell

'They sing the horizon,' my mother said, 'but all they have to offer is darkness.'

I was barely four the first time she told me this, stroking my forehead as I shivered off the remains of a fever in my corner of the attic. In the wavering uncertainty of illness and youth, my memories are jumbled out of order. She must have already told me the story of the Tidelings before delivering her warning, but I can't remember it. Her words to me then were the first to put shape to the music in my head: 'They sing the horizon,' she had said, and with a child's uncomplicated wisdom, I understood.

She kissed my forehead, and departed. I was left alone, staring up at the roof. The square skylight framed a patch of sky, freckled with stars.

I repeated her words out loud, and listened.

On the very edge of my hearing there came the whispering from the spiral of my ear, I could hear their song, as if the echo of the sea in a shell had been given melody and voice. When I closed my eyes I could see them on the edges of the harbour, rising up out of the water for long enough to call out to me, before dipping their heads back under to chase in spirals beneath the surface.

Until I grew older, their travel in my dreams would halt here, just outside the reaches of the town's lights. When I was seven my mother was still repeating her grave warning, growing ever more forbidding as she hammered the bread dough with her rolling pin; 'All they have to offer is darkness.' She was the town's schoolmistress and well practised at lacing her utterances with a tone of certain doom. She was feared amongst my peers for a ruthlessness covered only by the thinnest coatings of kindness, but all I ever heard in her voice when she spoke to them was certainty and strength. Her warnings of the Tidelings were another matter: there was something darker beneath it.

By eleven, I could identify what it was—fear.

I had long since stopped talking about the song of the Tidelings. As a child, I had thought, with no reason to assume otherwise, that the ocean whispered its seductions to everyone. On a few occasions I had asked my father what the song sounded like to him. He had looked pointedly away and shaken his head. 'It's not all of us that hear it,' he told me, and swung down his axe like a full stop. The wood split cleanly.

When, a few years later, I asked him again, he stopped what he was doing and sat down next to me. 'Jonah,' he told me, and I knew that he was serious. 'You need to forget about this. The song isn't real. Put it out of your mind.' He rested an unfamiliar hand on my shoulder. 'And for the sake of us all, don't tell your mother.'

A drop of water rolled slowly down the windowpane.

'Why not?'

In his silence, I thought I would get no answer. When he finally spoke, it was with the heaviness of an adult who believed his answer was beyond his child's understanding. 'Because she's afraid for you,' he told me. I furrowed my brow, and he sighed. 'No parent wants their child to be different,' he said, and returned firmly to his work.

I started to pretend. I didn't mention the song again. I began to grow taller, stronger. Before going to bed I would consider my face in the polished mirror, my imagination painting a beard across my jaw. I would once have tallied the bruises or scratches of the day, the dusting of mud, the tokens of the day's freedoms, but these days I measured up the angles, starting to feel a sense of shape and enticement about my features. I would tuck my hair behind my ears, and caution myself that when I lay down to sleep, I would not listen for the music.

As if challenging my denial, the song of the ocean magnified; gentle waves became breakers, morning tide turned pounding crescendo against the rocks. Worse still, when I closed my eyes at night, the Tidelings no longer circled in the sea on the edge of the light. Now they came crawling out of the waves on the shore, dragging their stunted lengths up the lamplit streets. I would hear their hoarse gasping as they drew near my window, the damp scrape of scaled flesh on the slates outside. Here the dream would end, until the night after I skipped worship at school, and they arrived at my window.

Tap.

Tap.

Tap.

I would lie and stare resolutely in the other direction, but on some nights the light would catch the window right. I would see their shadows cast across the boards, leaning over the skylight, clawed hand extended from the tangle of drowned hair, rapping a sharp knuckle against the glass. Then I would awaken with a start to the smell of salt and seaweed and their refrain reverberating around my head. Rising to look out the window, there was never anything but the circle of rocks, isolated in its remote twist of the bay and cast red by the warning eye of the lighthouse.

I took care not to let my unsettled nights spill into the rhythms of the day, going about in daylight the same as everyone else. I embarked on the caretaking of my grand illusion with great passion, and gradually the gaps between my mother's warnings of the Tidelings grew wider. I could never block the song from my ears at night, but in my dreams there was never more than the tapping on the window.

With my thirteenth birthday came the spirit of investigation; I began to do more than endure my singular gift and to wonder why it was placed upon me and me alone. There was little to go on: I searched the reliquaries in the church, the books in the school's library, even sneaked into my father's study to see if there was anything of use there. I considered, then rejected, rowing out to interrogate the lighthouse keeper. Treated with a sense of fear by the children of the town, he was occasionally seen stomping the streets in a bulky hooded coat and gnarled leather boots. Of deeper interest to me was the ability that both sanctified and isolated him in his lone tower: he was the only man to be able to cross the bay at night and live to tell the tale. Although this intrigued me, I could not muster the courage to travel to see him, and no opportunity arose to corner him in the town.

My investigations turned up only one other snippet, snatched through the cracks of my floorboards that lay above my father's study.

'They'll send him out there,' my mother was saying, answered by my father's indistinct rumble. 'They will, and I don't blame them. Why, it's not natural, is it?'

Again, my father's voice, muffled by the floorboards. I thought I caught the word 'parents', but I wasn't sure.

'They'll understand,' my mother said tartly.

This time, I caught my father's voice. 'Would you if it was Jonah?'

The space between me and my mother tightened with the pause that preceded her pronouncement. Then: 'I would, without a hesitation.'

My chest tightened. I knew what 'send him out there' meant. When the sun set on the last day of the month the prison gates would be opened, the month's haul of prisoners led out and pushed into a small bunch of rowing boats. They would be pushed out, oarless, to drift on the tide.

Then they would come—the Tidelings.

What happened next was unclear, but when the lighthouse keeper made his way across the waves in the dawn light, he would be dragging behind him a small armada of empty boats.

That night, I changed the dream.

There was the song, the crawling, the slithering, the tapping. Their shadows lurched across the floor, knocking for me. I sat up in bed, pushed the covers back, breathed in courage and turned around. The window was empty, the Tidelings' shadows dissipating into nothing but shaking tree branches. What I had thought was the whirl of hair was simply a coruscation of snow being whipped past my window, the start of a winter storm.

I arose, and went to the window, expecting to see the usual blank stretch of rock and sand, the glaring eye of the lighthouse warning ships away. The light caught the snow from one side, painting it a glimmering red, whilst from the other side there was the orange glow of the town's gas-lamps. Catching the light as it did, the snow wheeled with the same joy as New Year's fireworks. Then, squinting through the eddies, I could just make out, perched on the largest rock looking out to sea, a small dark figure.

The song arose in my ear, a piercing aria punctuated by that rhythmic tap tap tap. I dragged on my dressing gown over my pyjamas and crept barefoot down the stairs. On the porch I pushed my already-frozen feet into father's thick walking boots. The garden lay mute and blanketed, the world beyond the hedge vanished into whiteness. I made my way down the hill guided by the glow of each consecutive gas-lamp ahead, and I was put in mind of the other stories I had been told as a child by my mother: witless travellers lured from the road by faerie lights, or—and here I shivered from more than cold—those of the demons that cried out as if in need to lure travellers from the path.

The road from our house wound a full turn down the bay. As I approached sea-level, the figure was still there, hunched on the rocks. I moved quietly closer, and observed. It was a boy, close to my age, thinly dressed. He was barefoot, and whenever the waves struck the rock splashes of water would rain down on them.

Whilst I could feel the ice creeping into my bones, the grate of the cobbles through my feet, the bite of the wind on my rapidly numbing earlobes, the boy seemed apart from it all. The snow stopped at his skin; it wrapped him in a halo, picked him out in orange light, this lonely figure on a rock in the middle of a snow-storm.

His separateness drew me out into the open, threading a treacherous path out onto the spit. The town, the lighthouse, even the cobbles I had only a moment ago departed from vanished into the snowstorm. The boy did not turn his head, but I saw his shoulder blades tighten with the expectation of disturbance.

Wordlessly, I sat down next to him.

I feel the cold now, more intensely than I did that night. This is a cold marked out not by ice or snow, but by dread. The sun slipped away quietly and without remark tonight. The night is clear. The air is brittle with expectation. 'It'll be tonight,' the word goes, from cell to cell. 'They'll send us tonight.'

I know they're right. My window is higher than the rest, just high enough to see over the wall down to the bay, where I can see them lining up the boats.

I crouch in the corner and wrap my arms around my knees, listening for their song. Were they coming? I couldn't hear them.

'Can you hear them?' he asked me, staring straight ahead. Snowflakes were scattered in his hair and caught on his eyelashes. His skin looked fragile and pale, his lips starting to turn blue at the corners. 'Can you hear them?' he asked again, and I was startled away from my observation.

'The Tidelings?' I had forgotten that their song was what had awoken me and led me here; it had been whipped away by my discovery of the boy. I turned my gaze out towards the harbour, and listened. The song was still there, a lullaby skating keenly on the borders of the icy wind. 'I can hear them,' I told him. 'I hear them every night.'

He inclined his head and fixed his eyes on mine. His lip trembled. No sound escaped them, but I could have snatched the words from his mouth because they were welling up unannounced in my own too. 'You're the first person who's ever heard it too,' I wanted to say—no, shout, scream in delight—but to put syllables to the feeling felt leaden and clumsy.

For a moment I thought he was going to cry but then he looked away, back out to the harbour. We sat in silence together, watching the storm railing fiercely around us.

'What's your name?' I whispered into his ear.

Quietly and without comment he rested his head into the crook of my shoulder. 'Tobias,' he said, against my chest, and with the sound of the storm around us, I felt his voice through me rather than hearing it.

Leaning in closer so he would hear, I told him, 'I'm Jonah.'

'Jonah Bedloe.' A guard pushed me into a room already crammed shoulder to shoulder with inmates. The guard at the podium ticked off my name.

The air was sharp with fear, from convict and guard. From outside the main doors there was the sound of keys turning in the ancient locks. 'Time to move,' the guard announced, and the other scattered officers herded us towards the doors. At shoulder-height, I was jostled roughly this way and that. I turned and looked every which way, trying to see Tobias, sure that if I was here, he would be too. But I could see nothing other than the scared faces of the men around me as we were led out into the courtyard. For a second I caught a glimpse of a shorter head between shoulders. I thrust an arm through the gap to try and reach, but grabbed empty air, and then I was swept outside. The lighthouse glared at us from a distance and winter air assaulted us and wreathed our heads in clouded breath.

'This way,' intoned the guard tightly, and we followed him out of the gates, down towards the water.

I sought about again for a sight of Tobias, but there were many of us and it was dark. I accosted several of the other convicts, but each upon turning would be someone else. I fell behind as the route narrowed between two inward-leaning ivy-coloured walls. The wet leaves brushed past my hand, then for a brief moment I felt the warmth of fingers grip my hand, delicate and warm. Even before I'd turned the touch vanished, and all I caught was a shoulder vanishing between two hulking men as the way widened out once again.

I opened my mouth to shout out for him, but a different quiet had overcome the group.

'Bear witness,' spoke the guard, words ritually precise. 'First: Mr. Josiah Adlard. You stand judged. Thievery and a breaking of the code of honesty amongst all good people. Step forward.'

A caved-in ruin of a man with wild hair and unkempt beard stepped forward. His clawed hands shook. 'Step into the boat, Josiah Adlard.'

A second guard led the man to the water's edge where the rowing boats were tethered. His feet fumbled to gain purchase as he was pushed into the boat and he fell sprawling into the bottom. The guard untied the rope from its post and pushed, and Mr. Josiah Adlard, Thief, was slowly borne away from the cluster of boats and out to sea. I watched his face receding, staring back at us with a cobwebby confusion.

'Second: Master Jonah Bedloe.' Hands on my shoulders pushed me forward. For a second time, I thought I felt the brush of fingertips against my palm but couldn't turn to look. I tried to stop my feet from tripping and to arrive in front of the guard with some dignity.

'You have been judged,' he said.

My arm was around Tobias, sheltering his body as best I could from the cold. He wasn't shivering, didn't seem to register the cold, despite the fact that his arm was freezing to the touch.

'It's getting louder,' he shouted to me, so lost in the noise that it might as well have been a whisper.

'I can hear it,' I shouted back, and it was true. The Tidelings' song was louder, purer, coming at us from every angle of the night. With every crash of the ocean against the rock another melody was thrown towards us. I tightened my grip around him, and hunched myself, feeling his closeness against me.

There came an abrupt crescendo of waves. A wall of water erupted, thrown up from the meeting of the sea and the rocks. It seemed to hang in the air, then poured down on us. I could picture us from far-away, how we might look from my bedroom window where I had first spied him, two tiny figures in the centre of a snowstorm, christened by the leaping waters of the sea itself.

We scrabbled back, pulled ourselves from the edge, fell in a tangle of limbs into a dell of rock. Another wave dashed itself to death and the sky rained down again. The Tidelings' song rose up louder, drawn from the seabed by the waves themselves, as if every droplet that poured down onto our bodies contained the notes of the music. The music soared, reaching a final high, piercing note.

We fell into each other as the song broke around us.

'They sing the horizon,' my mother had said, but the horizon was dark, barely more than a slight shift from black to a yet deeper black. The only thing truly visible was the blazing of the scarlet lighthouse. On either side of me drifted the boats, spread across the still surface like leaves on the surface of a pond. The men were arranged in various tableaux of fear: crouched clutching their legs or frantically windmilling their arms in the water in a bid to row their boats, or standing like pirate captains in the sterns, seeking around for signs of liberation.

I sat in the belly of the boat and looped my wrist through the empty oarlocks. In either direction I could see perhaps three or four boats clearly, and then the mirages of more beyond.

The tide would drift us closer then further apart as the minutes washed away. Occasionally, a convict would shout something. A regret, a curse, an apology. For the most part the others ignored them, for although we might be sailing like a small pathetic fleet, each of us felt in our bones our aloneness in facing what was to come.

And then, one cry taken up along the line.

'They are coming. The Tidelings are coming.'

There was a stillness, in which the wind died down, and the snow stopped its desperate dance and became instead a calm drift. Our faces drew apart, and we examined every detail of each other, as if to draw a map. Snow and ice crept paths over his face, and his blue eyes reflected the whiteness around us. So detached, so separate, I imagined him as the very child of winter, come to me out of the blizzard.

For an unmeasurable time, the world stopped at our skin. Then came the voices, and sweeping of lantern beams, and the intrusion of others.

'They're coming,' I whispered in his ear.

'They are coming. The Tidelings are coming!' I could hear the call in the far distance to my left and right. I knelt in the bow of the boat, and stared out towards the horizon.

In the next boat along, one of the other convicts, Mr Jack Wainwright, Public Drunkard, was covering his ears and openly weeping. 'Can you hear the song?' he wailed to me across the water.

I shook my head and looked back to the horizon. I could still see nothing, and more importantly I could hear nothing. 'They sing the horizon, but all they have to offer is darkness,' my mother had said, and in and amongst her warnings there had been other grimly muttered facts. 'No man can resist them,' she had told me. 'You mind yourself.'

In the direction of the horizon, I saw the first crestings. From where I was they were just brief flickers, as if whales or sharks were surfacing for air. I took up the cry. 'They're coming! I can see them. They're coming for us!'

As I watched, the darting of fins drew nearer, and with it a deep, forbidding chanting. I threw myself down into the meagre protection of the boat. This was not the song I was used to: usually the curl of notes contained the promise of choice and happiness. Now the tune had cankered and rotted, still ringing of promises, but now those of the infernally inevitable. I clung to the oarlocks and prayed.

I saw Jack kneeling in his boat, peering over the side. Drawn to watch, I saw her rise.

The Tideling arose from the ocean, water pouring off her. Her hair cascaded down then spread itself into the water, waving loosely. Her face and neck were a translucent blue, webbed with delicate white veins. I could not properly see her face, but Jack's was transfixed upon her, mouth hanging loosely open. She raised her hand to his face, stroked it, webbed fingers tracking across his skin. Her body arched against the side of the boat, thrusting against the wooden sides. Blackened lips kissed his neck, crept upwards. She threw back her head, bent backwards, breasts exposed to him, drawing his hands out of the vessel with her. Jack ran a hand down her neck, around the curves of her chest. The boat tipped dangerously towards the surface of the water. The Tideling drew herself close for the final seduction. I could hear sounds issuing from her mouth, and whilst I could not interpret their meaning, I could read the crazed ecstasy in Jack's face. His hands were drawn lower, below the surface of the water.

A blink later and he was gone. The boat tipped past the point of no return and he plunged into the water, with only time for a final gurgled scream. The Tideling raised herself ferociously out of the water, fully exposed to me. For the second that she was posed like this she seemed to have changed from the beauty of moments before. The palms of her hand curdled into obscene suckers like the dead octopi that had washed up on the shores after a storm. Her hair was a tangle of seaweed and driftwood and her open mouth spewed rotten bilgewater that ran down her body to where her sex mutated into glinting black scales. She snarled and then dived, and all I could hear was my mother's words floating back to me. 'They can offer only darkness,' she said, and then Jack and the Tideling were gone.

From across the scattered boats, I could hear the mingled sounds of drowning breath and seductive song. I saw Josiah Adlard dragged into the water with a priapic grin of lust upon his face. Again, my mother's voice: 'No man can resist, Jonah.'

Then it all stopped, and she arose at the stern.

At first eyes, fixing me, beckoning me. Her full face was raised up on a slender neck and shoulders. I fell to my knees and crawled towards her, as she opened her mouth and sang to me.

I cannot give words to the song, except to tell of what it promised. Of possession, and manhood, the Tideling sang. We would swim beneath the waves, chase the scent of freedom, dash in spirals of abandon, and on the ocean bed I would tower over her and take her with an easy strength. She would be mine. She whispered of a world of pleasure I had never experienced, spoke of a birthright I was being denied. She rose up from the water, locked her hands behind my head. *Come into the horizon,* she sang. *Come...*

Her hand parted my shirt and traced over my chest. She grasped my hands and drew them to wet skin. Rising further, back arched, she fully displayed her womanhood.

Come into the horizon, continued the song.

Tobias had been picked out in silhouette by the lights of the lanterns criss-crossing from the foot of the hill towards us. We climbed to our feet, pulled each other close and clasped our hands, as the figures of my parents and others I had never seen before strode across the rocks to pull him away.

My mother grabbed his shoulders and yanked him away. She reached out to me, seized me by the wrists and dragged me behind her. Ahead, I saw the face of my father, stricken with confusion, before I was drawn quickly past. Tobias was being similarly dragged by a man I took to be his father.

I felt again the feeling of Tobias' head resting against my shoulder with my arm wrapped around in protection. Warmth burst inside my chest where his head had rested, and I broke the grip on my wrists. My mother stumbled back, and turned to me with anger writ large across her face. She fumbled to return her grasp, and on that boat in the night, with the same fury nakedly apparent, the Tideling drew back into the water. She hissed and spat foul-smelling liquid at me. The song lashed out at me, hurling me images of myself, pathetic, weak, reviled, isolated, but I ignored her and drew myself to my knees.

Then she was gone, and there was nothing but silence on the sea. Empty boats bobbed listlessly around me. One, thrown by a force I tried not to imagine, drifted up against mine, and tapped against it.

I sank back into the bottom of the boat, and waited, unsure of what to do. I was one boy alone in a boat on the ocean, but somehow the feeling was familiar.

Time passed—perhaps an hour or so—and I heard the splash of oars. From the direction of the lighthouse came a boat, larger than my own, swiftly cutting through the water towards me. Drawing closer, I could make out the lighthouse keeper, a huge coil of rope looped around his shoulder. The only man to go out at night and survive—out of what had once been a childish monster-under-the-bed fear of him, I felt the beginnings of understanding and a strange kinship.

He guided his vessel across the sea, pausing beside each discarded boat, looping his rope through the ring in the stern and dragging it behind him. With the first fingers of dawn picked out his route across towards me, he had the look of a swan swimming serenely through the waters with a gaggle of clumsy ducklings following behind. By the time he had reached me there were nigh on twenty boats behind him, and I was sure I must be his final catch of the day.

In hailing distance, he raised his hat with a politeness that jarred with the setting. 'Evening,' he said, and reached into his boat. 'You'll be one of them ones.'

I gazed at him dumbly.

'I wouldn't go so far as to say lucky,' he said, 'but something like that.' From the bottom of his boat he hauled a pair of oars. 'Here,' he grunted, and extended them to me.

I didn't stop to question, and scrambled to pull them into my boat.

'What do I do now?' I asked him. 'I don't understand—how did I—how did you—I thought that all men...'

'I don't have your answers, lad.'

'But—so—you and me...'

The lighthouse keeper raised a hand and pointed over his shoulder. 'Not just me, and not just you,' he said.

Another boat floated out of the dark. The glimmering of dawn, like the spirals of snow in lantern light when I had first seen him, cast a bright halo around him. 'Tobias!' I shouted out, and he looked up at me, a wide smile lighting his face. He fell to his knees and threw out his hand as far as he could towards me.

'You see,' said the lighthouse keeper. He gave the edge of my boat a push, and then began to row himself away. I drifted closer toward Tobias and I stretched out my arm to him and his beaming face.

Our hands drifted closer, hands closer and closer to meeting. Behind me, rowing away towards his silent, still lighthouse, the lighthouse keeper shouted out to us, 'Just keep rowing, into the horizon, until you're free.'

Take Out the Trash
Bob Smith

Peggy made me laugh when she confessed, 'Real vanity is dyeing your chemo stubble blonde to keep from going gray.' She nodded her oddly attractive, bristly head before adding, 'Mark and Jacob would never get that. No one healthy would. And I could never tell them that a life-threatening illness makes you feel like a vampire since you spend a part of every day in your coffin.'

She was referring to our husbands, the sweetest, most thoughtful guys imaginable. We had to be guarded with our gallows humor around them since our families needed to pretend the elephant in the room isn't dying. Peggy and I were having our expensive, weekly Friday lunch at the Gramercy Tavern, where we always split a bottle of wine. By the end of the meal, I had to pull out my iPad to converse since my illness makes my tongue tipsy, and imbibing even one glass of vino makes me sound blotto.

Peggy has ovarian cancer, and I have what — in the rest if the English-speaking world — is sensibly named motor neuron disease. Here in the United States, it's called Lou Gehrig's disease, which makes it sound like some ad agency believed an endorsement by a famous baseball player would make everyone line up to get an illness that kills most people within three to five years.

Peggy Berger and I have been best friends since we met in our late twenties at a very dull cocktail party where the only snack was mixed nuts. We reached for the same bowl, and mid-grab, she said, 'This is the most puritanical treat in the world; its message is, 'whatever you love, there will never be enough of it.' '

We were both single then and I replied, 'It's like dating. You have to munch a lot of filberts and Brazil nuts before you'll meet a cashew.'

A version of our conversation appeared in Peggy's first novel. She lives with her dentist husband Jacob and their two college-age sons on the Upper West Side on 96th, while I live in the Village on MacDougal between Houston and Bleecker with Mark and our dog Argos. Mark studied ancient Greek literature at Columbia, but now sells real estate, which turns out to be the odyssey of many classics majors. Peggy's a successful comic novelist who's been called the Jewish Barbara Pym. Her main characters are always involved with a Reform temple and keep kosher at home, but order the shrimp shumai at Chinese restaurants and have loads of gay and lesbian friends.

I own an antique shop in the East Village that specializes in fifties furniture, with an emphasis on Heywood-Wakefield. The last time Peggy visited my shop, she suggested I should be buried in a boomerang-shaped coffin, which made me laugh on a day when my doctor informed me my breathing capacity had diminished by ten percent. New Yorkers with life-threatening illnesses regard the Angel of Death as the meanest and most despicable landlord ever. He's trying to evict us from our affordable, sunny billion-room apartments for a six-feet-under, windowless basement studio. Peggy found out about her illness five months before my first symptoms appeared. Nine months later, when I received my you're-gonna-die-agnosis, Peggy's first response was, 'Eric, do you have to copy everything I do?'

The best thing about our lunches is we often don't discuss our health.

'*Fanny and Alexander* is playing at Film Forum next week,' Peggy said. Bergman's masterpiece was our favorite Christmas movie — the five-hour mini-series, not the three-hour feature — and the two of us always watched it together every December. We decided to see the first part Friday night and the second on Saturday during the day. 'Let's go to Bareburger,' I said. It was our favorite burger joint where everything was organic, including the ketchup and mustard. Junk food is as popular in Manhattan as in the rest of the country, but New Yorkers like to delude ourselves that our

French fries gleam with a slick cosmopolitan sheen while others are just greasy.

Peggy informed me that she was reading this year's massive literary novel overpraised by the *New York Times* – written by the latest in a long line of white, heterosexual male authors, men who possess a deep understanding of the hardships that successful, white, heterosexual males have to endure, and who express their anguish with perfectly crafted baseball, boxing, or bullfighting metaphors.

'It's a snooze,' she declared. 'Critics should be required to have a life-threatening illness. Then, when something's praised, you'd know it's worth your time.'

'Yeah,' I said. 'I can't wait to read, 'This movie is worth seeing if you have two years to live, but if you only have three months, I'd pass.''

There was a much longer-than-usual delay in Peggy's response. Her pause suggested that something was wrong. People want to believe knowing that you're about to die confers wisdom. Well, I hate to disillusion everyone, but beyond knowing that I might be dead soon — and I keep hoping I'm wrong about that too — my life still sometimes seems as hazy as my afterlife.

'How are you doing?'

'I don't know. My doctor thinks my cancer might have spread. I'm seeing a specialist at Sloan-Kettering on Monday.'

I grabbed her hand. We both felt the unspoken bond that we each knew what the other was going through: an affiliation I cherished, since most of the people who knew what we were going through could no longer tell us what they were going through.

You see, we weren't in denial. No one with a life-threatening illness is in denial. If we don't speak about it, we're probably being considerate and believe *you* can't handle that conversation. When someone terminally-ill doesn't feel like chatting about funeral arrangements, a realistic explanation for their reluctance is that they understand living is a full-time job, while dying is a vacation.

You're forced to confront that as much you like to think you're indispensable, you're not. People and things will go on without you, so you might as well relax and try to enjoy yourself. A terminal illness imparts the freedom to be selfish without guilt since you'll soon be one of the selfless, unneedy dead. Neither Peggy nor I were religious. I felt that every prayer was an instant message and the reply was always the same: 'God's not online right now.'

'What can I do to help?'

'Have lunch with me after my appointment.'

Of course, I agreed, thinking Mondays were slow and I could afford to take a two-hour lunch. Peggy's smile drooped. Unfortunately one of the cruelest side effects of any life-threatening illness is that it physically alters its victims' faces — weaker muscles and slacker flesh — until they perpetually look like they're mourning the loss of their own lives. We both watched as the maitre d' seated the unbearable portly television host of a so-called news program at a nearby table. His mean-spirited shows only featured one story: his own lack of charity. Peggy put down her wine glass. 'Why do decent people get diseases like biblical punishments while that evil fat fuck thrives?'

I was feeling the wine and said, 'Every person on earth with a life-threatening illness should threaten the life of one evil person.'

'You're right,' said Peggy. 'The fear of God is too immaterial, but the fear of an angry cancer patient — that's palpable.'

Our discussion of life-and-death matters was jocular but serious — as the humor of seriously ill people always is. But I began to be excited by our idea and thought it might be one last gift the dying could leave to posterity.

'If you have a terminal illness, what's wrong with taking out the sickest fucks on the planet?' I asked. 'I wouldn't advise a healthy person to try to kill these scumbags, but someone with a fatal disease — what are they going to do to him or her? A death sentence would come off as euthanasia compared to dying from Lou Gehrig's disease or ovarian cancer.'

Peggy laughed. 'Take out the trash before you go!'

I was impressed by her perfect summation of our conversation, but she was a writer and it made sense. We stopped our lighthearted musing about murder and asked for the check. It shocked me that I didn't feel bad about the thought of killing malignant people, even though I was against the death penalty in America, where the darker your skin, the greater your chances of facing the black interior of a casket paid for by the good people of Texas.

Peggy and I left the restaurant, but for the rest of the day I kept considering all the horrors of the living dead — the terminally ill killing despicable people — like zombies with a strong sense of right and wrong. I weighed that people often can't agree on who's loathsome, but figured putting the fear of retribution out there with an unending supply of the terminally ill could transform the world. The ancient Greeks believed in the Furies, winged snake-haired avengers of injustice with blood dripping from their eyes. But they also called them the Eumenides, 'the Kindly Ones.' I wasn't sure why they called them that, but I liked to believe it stemmed from a conviction that sometimes, ruthless vengeance is an act of philanthropy. For over two thousand years, the Furies hadn't been watching our backs. Who has a clearer vision about life than someone watching it slip away?

Later that night, I was checking out Facebook, reading the status updates of my friends, thinking, 'Really, Gavin? Do we need to know you're going to the gym? Doesn't your shirtless profile photo tell us that when you're not home or at work, you're lifting weights?'

Peggy IMed me. 'I've been thinking about our conversation.'

'Me too.'

'I think we should do it.'

I'm embarrassed to say I typed in a happy face emoticon.

Peggy typed, 'We shouldn't discuss this online. Only in person.'

It took me a second to realize what we were advocating could bring us to the attention of Homeland Security.

'When do you want to meet?'

'Tomorrow,' she typed.

Peggy and I met almost every other day for the next three weeks. We divided up the tasks. Peggy wrote the manifesto for our movement, and I acquired the domain name www.takeoutthetrash.com. It took me awhile to figure out how to register it in Belarus, which I learned was the nation where shady websites sought refuge. It also took weeks for me to find all the websites in English dealing with life-threatening illnesses. Peggy researched all the sites in French and Spanish, the two foreign languages in which she was fairly fluent. Our plan was to place our manifesto all over the Web in a day, while remaining untraceable, posting from Internet cafes on cheap refurbished laptops we'd use once then toss.

There were numerous conversations about how we might be inciting right-wing assassins to kill good people. I argued that they killed Martin Luther King without our website and that our appeal should be directed to terminally ill agnostics and atheists who I thought would feel freer to kill without God looking over their shoulders. Peggy said, 'If we start this war against the wicked, probably some good people will die.'

'Good people die every day and in every war against the bad. I feel that the altruistic urge to sacrifice yourself to help others will appeal more to people who actually spent time when they were healthy thinking about the plight of others. Most right-wing conservatives care more about their wallets than people, and when they're dying I bet they spend all their time trying to convince themselves that their imminent move to heaven is a good thing since it's an exclusive, restricted gated community.'

Peggy laughed. 'You might be right.'

We also discussed not just being passive, guilty-as-charged domestic terrorists and resolved to make an effort to take out one piece of trash ourselves. Since Peggy was too busy dealing with her worsening health, we decided I would buy a gun and take shooting lessons. My illness had weakened my grip strength, and it took me awhile to find a weapon that didn't require a powerful trigger finger.

Thankfully, gun-store owners are very thoughtful and considerate about their customers' needs. Bud Farley, owner of Farley's Guns, listened attentively as I explained my problem and then prescribed an M16 automatic rifle whose trigger pulled with such ease that even the Angel of Death, with his bony grip, could comfortably fire off a round. I practiced at a shooting range in New Jersey, and it turned out I had an aptitude for ending lives prematurely. I went twice a week, telling Mark I was going for Reiki treatments.

Peggy and I had long discussions about whom I was going to kill. There are so many people who deserve to die that choosing just one seemed unfair to the other monsters of the earth. We settled on Reverend Bix because people of all political and religious faiths regarded him as ecumenically evil. He was the minister in Waco, Texas whose church picketed gay and military funerals with 'God Hates Fags' signs. I even worried that if I didn't pick him off on the day our manifesto was posted, someone else would kill him first, since he was such an obvious target.

I researched his life as well as I could online and then actually flew out to Waco beforehand to scope him out. It turned out that he rarely ventured out of his church compound, perhaps since it seemed everyone in his hometown hated him too. I mentioned his name in a diner, and my waitress immediately snapped, 'The cheap bastard. He believes tipping in restaurants is a form of usury condemned in the Bible.' By chance, I was lurking outside his compound pondering ways to ambush him, when I learned from his mail carrier that he went to see a podiatrist once a month due to bunions and chronic athlete's foot. Killing him at his doctor's office seemed doable, I thought, while boarding my plane back to New York. (I had lied again and told Mark that someone in Waco was selling a house full of pristine, original wheat-finish Heywood-Wakefield, and it was too good a deal to pass up. I hated my dishonesty, but planning a murder forces you to do some unsavory things.)

We posted our manifesto shortly after I returned. The first line was, 'We, the terminally ill people, want to make the world healthier by ridding our planet of sick fucks.' At first, there wasn't much significant reaction, although numerous negative comments were immediately posted by people who believed in Jesus but who clearly had no idea how to spell Pontius Pilate. It seems that we initially escaped the government's attention by posting on sites like www.coughingupblood.com that were read only by people with life-threatening illnesses. But we knew our message was getting across when Peggy found and sent me the link for a YouTube video of a dark-haired young man named Jorge Torres. In his twenties, he was hooked up to an oxygen tank and had memorized the entire manifesto and recited it to the camera with a surprisingly forceful and moving delivery.

The night before I left for Waco, Peggy and I had dinner at the Gramercy Tavern. She looked much worse, a skeleton who frowned occasionally, and she only ordered a crab cake appetizer, which she picked at in a desultory fashion. We both knew it would be the last time we'd see each other. Peggy would soon be a writer saying her last words and after I shot Reverend Bix I'd be going to jail. It was sad, but Peggy smiled as she lifted her one glass of wine in a toast. 'Here's to not going gently into that good night.' I clinked her glass and said, 'We're definitely not doing that.'

I'd arranged to buy another gun online in Waco and would pick it up there. I could have packed and flown with a weapon, but my hands were growing progressively weaker, and I traveled then with just a knapsack since getting even a small suitcase off the luggage carousel was an ordeal. The entire journey had a surreal quality. I felt that I was concealing a murderer who was having cold-blooded second thoughts. Before we took off, the fat, chatty old woman seated next to me on the flight to Dallas admitted that she was afraid of flying. She probably wouldn't have appreciated my taking her mind off her fear by telling her that she was sharing an armrest with someone afraid that he lacked the courage to murder a hateful reverend.

Peggy and I were staying in touch via iPads; I had jokingly called them 'diePads' one time, but we both mercifully buried my groaner by never mentioning it again. She had been sending me messages every hour to buck up my will-to-kill. One had been particularly helpful:

'Eric, I know it's hard to think of yourself as a killer. No, make that impossible. We were raised to think of murderers as villains and always imagined that the worst crime we'd ever commit would involve repaying our debt to society with a check to the parking bureau. But you never imagined that one day you'd be a man with motor neuron disease. I remember when you told me that you once read about your illness years ago and that you clearly recalled thinking, 'That has to be one of the most horrible diseases that could happen to anyone.' You've handled that unimaginable misery with exceptional grace and good humor, and now you have to shoulder another previously undreamed-of, unfair burden. Some people pick up litter as their community service, but unfortunately you have to take out the trash.'

It was actually easy to find out what day Reverend Bix was going to see his podiatrist. I called the office pretending to be one of his sons saying we had lost his appointment card and were confused about the date. I figured the receptionist would tell me, since the reverend's children were treated like indentured servants, and Bix wouldn't waste his valuable hate-filled time checking on a medical appointment when he could order one of his kids to do it.

I waited in my car in Dr. Kim's parking lot for Reverend Bix to show up. I could still drive as I had the bulbar variant of motor neuron disease where the legs are the last to go. Now that I was actually poised to kill him, my doubts intensified. Was killing evil people the answer? Couldn't the justice of our arguments change malicious minds? My brain gunned down that pipe dream after fruitlessly trying to think of an example in history when that had ever happened.

A black van pulled into the parking lot with a plain, young redheaded woman behind the wheel. I'd Google-imaged Bix, so when her graying red-haired father got out of the passenger side, I immediately recognized his nasty face. Reverend Bix was the kind of congenital 'Christian' prick who probably suspects angels are fags for wearing feathers. My M16 sat on my lap.

When the time came, I felt sorry for Reverend Bix and his daughter and thought I couldn't go through with it. But then I remembered all the mothers and grandmothers who had the worst day of their lives — burying a child — made even worse by him. For the first time, I considered the paradox that in order to do some real good in the world, you need to be as heartless as the people who inflict pain.

I also thought of my sweet Mark. He had never complained about all the small and big things he needed to do as I got sicker: helping me with buttons and zippers, opening jars and bottles, going with me to the doctor's when I was scared. I wanted him to remember me as his witty, handsome husband, not as a carcass who needed to bathed, fed, and wiped. He deserved a world free of people like Bix, and I would rather die in jail than put Mark through the horror of watching me die in a hospice. Then I thought about Peggy. Life had already cruelly betrayed her, and now I was thinking of letting her down again. I got out of my car, aimed at Bix's chest — so his brains wouldn't splatter on his daughter — and pulled the trigger.

Mark was furious when he learned his husband was a murderer — pissed that Peggy and I hadn't asked him to be an accomplice, angrier than when I forgot to buy his favorite nonfat Greek yogurt at Trader Joe's. But in gay relationships, it seems that killing someone horrible is easier to forgive than cheating with someone desirable. After a few months, Mark regarded my breaking the Thou shalt not kill rule as going off my diet. Ice cream and homicide were temptations, but he'd overlook my lapse if I vowed to have more willpower in the future.

Peggy entered hospice two days before I was sentenced. Our last phone call was a knife in my heart as she still was sharp, but her voice was very weak. She came close to being indicted as a coconspirator, but the DA thought, 'What's the point?' and let her off. Peggy was happy. Though, that the *Times* did credit her as the creator of the phrase, 'Take Out The Trash Before You Go.' She said, 'If that's how I get in *Bartlett's*, I'll take it.'

My favorite prison guard Walter is in his fifties, and his grim, wrinkled face makes it appear that even his childhood freckles were just prepubescent liver spots. I've decided most middle-aged men look as if they've been punked every night in their forties by gangs of teenage boys throwing rolls of flab over their skeletons while they slept.

'Good morning, Eric. How are you feeling?'

His turkey neck and slight paunch unfortunately reminded me of myself, while I probably reminded him of his father who died of motor neuron disease about two years ago.

'Good,' I answered, but Walter's face flickered with incomprehension. My voice is at the stage where I have to repeat everything, but Walter knows the drill and just says, 'I'm sorry. I didn't catch that.' It's always said with a mournful inflection that seems to register that both of us are losing hope as my voice continues to deteriorate.

'GOOD,' I said once more, trying to enunciate the word with a forced clarity. Walter's face visibly relaxed, a sign that he understood me. Even small talk now was a daredevil feat, clearly enunciating 'hello' had become a mouth-gaping accomplishment.

'I'm going to have a visitor tomorrow,' I added, knowing I sounded mentally retarded, but trying not to become angry since I often thought my friends and family were imbeciles when they couldn't understand me.

'Your mother?' Walter asked.

'Yes,' I said, sounding like I was trying to talk with a mouth full of pebbles.

My two brothers Leo and Carl had stopped speaking to me after I murdered Reverend Bix. My mom's different. She was already disappointed when the universe gave her a son with motor neuron disease; then when it gave her a murderous son, it was just more pain she had to endure. She was angry and confused after I was arrested and then became ashamed when newspaper, magazine, and television reporters showed up at her front door. Later, my mom asked if what they were saying was true: that I was the mastermind behind the whole Take Out The Trash movement. I admitted that I was half of it. She erupted, 'You don't go around killing people just because you don't like them! Are you crazy?'

Unfortunately for her, and them, I wasn't crazy — even though every day I mulled over the possibility that I could be insane. But I always reached the same verdict that the court-ordered psychologists had reached: Not Nuts. My mom lives in my hometown of Cleveland, and flying to Texas is an ordeal for a seventy-seven-year-old woman with a bum knee. On her last visit, she finally asked how this whole thing started.

'Let's not do that,' I said.

'I want to know,' she said, her blue eyes burning like gas flames.

My mother is stoic, and I knew she could handle it. I still felt guiltier about making her the mother of a son with a motor neuron disease than making her the mother of a murderer, but she deserved an explanation. You don't gun down a so-called minister without giving it some thought. I wanted my mom to understand that my decision to kill Reverend Bix was entirely premeditated. She listened patiently as I told her about my relationship with Peggy, who my mom adored, and explained our rationale that only dying men and women could make the world better.

Take Out the Trash started slowly but soon metastasized around the world. Peggy lived long enough to watch the nonstop coverage from London about a young man dying from a fatal melanoma who hid a bomb in his wheelchair and blew himself up while being blessed by the Pope. The investigation into Ryan McConnell's past brought to light years of sexual abuse by priests in Ireland, which the church covered up. A fat, viciously homophobic radio personality was poisoned by a gay waiter who put cyanide in the caramelized topping of his crème brûlée. It was revealed later that the waiter had pancreatic cancer.

The movement became the subject of a presidential address to the nation after three patients from a cancer ward in DC murdered two Supreme Court justices who had voted to give health insurance companies more rights to influence elections than sick Americans would ever have. And it was no surprise when the head of the National Rifle Association was gunned down by a grandmother in the early stages of Alzheimer's. Her grandson had been paralyzed by a bullet from a mentally ill sniper who shot him while he was walking to school. That's when talk about banning the terminally ill from buying guns was proposed in Congress by hard-core Second Amendment fanatics. A middle-aged man with 'popcorn lungs' whose second lung transplant was failing committed one of the first of many corporate murders. He shot the CEO of a microwave popcorn company after recently released memos and e-mails revealed the company had known for years that breathing in the artificial butter flavoring was harmful.

Most 'Trashers,' as they were called in the press, freely confessed at their trials that their lethal actions had been inspired by our manifesto, but others didn't want to upset their families. (I guess it's hard to maintain your stature as a responsible adult when you can successfully resist online appeals for money from Nigeria, but can't resist a website that advocates murder.) When the orange-skinned Speaker of the House refused to acknowledge global warming, it initially seemed like an accident when, a week later, he died trapped in a tanning booth with a broken OFF switch and a missing doorknob on the inside. But the police investigation eventually pointed to a stalker with lymphoma who had two children and was a member of several environmental groups.

Peggy and I had been afraid that our manifesto could encourage killings over minor transgressions; a bus driver might be knifed for expressing annoyance when requested to operate the wheelchair lift. But there haven't been any incidents of that type so far. Seems like most terminally ill people do gain a sense of what's really important about life. It struck me as hopeful when it was reported that the ex-governor of Alaska and her picnicking family had been chased by sharpshooting animal rights activists (each with various fatal illnesses) from helicopters. Staying true to the activists' beliefs, no one was killed, and after being harried for five miles, the ex-governor held a press conference announcing that maybe animals shouldn't be hunted from aircraft.

My mother listened intently and was silent after I'd finished. I knew she was concerned about my soul. Every Sunday, my mother went to mass at a Catholic church and maintained her tenuous faith by choosing to believe God was like every other man in her life — basically a good guy who would deeply and repeatedly hurt and disappoint her. She shrugged. 'This wouldn't have happened if God didn't give you your disease.'

I didn't mention that if her loving God gave me my illness, then he was trash too.

'If I get to heaven and you're not there, oh, I'm going to give God a piece of mind.'

I laughed at the thought of my mother hectoring God. She would never let up and would quickly make the Almighty understand the drawbacks of eternity.

'It's not funny,' she said. 'It's His fault.'

All I could conclude was that it was good for an agnostic to have a backup plan — and reassuring since I had complete faith that she would never let God   forget that our father who art in heaven was a deadbeat dad who ignored his kids' cries for help for millions of years.

I've been in jail for two years now, waiting to be executed, and thought the Take Out the Trash movement would have petered out by now. It hasn't. However the killings have become less frequent since just the threat of slaughter by the terminally ill is usually enough to force people to be more humane. A congressman recently proposed cutting food stamps, while maintaining subsidies for oil companies, but, after his family shied away from appearing in public with such an obvious target, he reconsidered and withdrew his proposal.

The movement shows no signs of dying. It's given people who've been shown the door a sense of purpose and even hope. Wheelchairs proudly sport bumper stickers saying 'Garbage Truck,' and before every session of Congress it's become customary for people with life-threatening illnesses to march or be pushed in front of the Capitol waving trash bags. There will invariably be a few people who will try to slip back into mean, selfish, uncaring ways, but sick people are as plentiful as germs. Fortunately, it's not always apparent who's dealing with a life-threatening illness, so the heinous get taken out before long. And my brothers have started visiting me. They've both had health scares – Leo barely survived a massive heart attack and Carl had what they suspected might be adrenal cancer, but turned out to be a symptom of the two pots of coffee he guzzled every day.

There is no natural change of seasons in prison; you only know that summer's arrived when the weekend sun bakes the guards' doughy faces to a flakey brown. While walking in the yard, the dust on the asphalt reminds me that I'll soon be in the ground, exchanging a comparatively spacious prison cell for eternal solitary confinement. I often wonder about God — even we agnostics believe in thinking about Him — and I ask myself what kind of by-the-book merciless judge sentences everyone — even children — to that cruel-and-usual punishment?

The prison chaplain left another Bible in my cell while I was in the yard. I gave it back, telling him that God was a shady politician who wrote his self-serving memoirs but refused to submit to a tough Q and A.

My outburst made me long for Peggy. She would have laughed.

Wear Your Love Like Heaven
Cody Quijano-Schell

Rudy hurried out the front door, coffee in one hand, a file in the other. His folded up jacket was under one arm and he pulled the door shut with his foot, careful not to scuff his dress shoes. He went to lock the door realizing his keys were in the pockets of his jacket.

'Gah!' It was a random noise he made in moments of frustration. It was probably a leftover from his parents training him not to yell 'God Dammit' every time something annoyed him. Just 'Gah!' perfectly expressed that same feeling. Rudy was balancing his coffee on the mailbox when a voice from behind surprised him.

'I *know* about your husband.' It was the man from across the street. He was the owner of the house with the flagpole. Old Glory was, as always, flying without fail.

Rudy felt his stomach knot. He was afraid of this. An openly gay couple moving into the neighborhood was bound to raise some eyebrows. 'Yes, that's right. My name is Rudy, his is Omran. We're married just like any other couple.'

The man frowned, hesitating only briefly before accepting the offered handshake. 'Nice to meet you, Rudy. I'm Keith.'

Rudy was annoyed that this was happening already. 'Everyone knows about my husband. It's not a secret. Our entire families were at the wedding.' Rudy felt guilty about this slight fib.

'I don't mean that you're... homosexuals. That's your business. I've been watching. I know his *other* secret.'

The color drained from Rudy's face. 'I don't know what you mean. And I have to get to work!' He pushed past Keith and hurried to the car.

Keith followed Rudy's car as it backed out. 'I hope you know what you're involved with. I hope you know what he *is*!'

Rudy's hand was shaking as he turned on the radio. The voices instantly annoyed him and he switched it off, quickly. *How could he know?*

Omran stood near the edge of the rooftop and took a sip of coffee. Light was sneaking up, overtaking the city. At this time of the morning, everything was brown, blue and grey. Between the brown brick buildings and under the bluish gray sky there were no solid shadows, nor any instances of shining brightness. It made everything seem flat, like an amateur photo. It felt unreal.

It was also unreal that Omran was going to let his family meet Rudy. He had already played out dozens of scenarios, none realistically positive, which frankly exhausted him. But it was time for them to meet.

Omran tipped his cup up to finish off the last of his coffee. The dark brown circle swirled into a stranger shape and rushed out of view as he swallowed. A plain white circle remained in the bottom of the cup.

There it was again: Geometry. The way liquid behaves in different containers was entrancing to Omran. Despite being an architect, solid shapes held little interest for him. His fascination with the way light, air, people and sound interacted in the completed structure was what made him brilliant at his job.

The sun was finally up. Omran looked down and saw a young boy walking west. It was funny the way it looked like the boy was pushing his shadow as he walked. Shadows look natural from every direction, except for when one is travelling away from the light.

Omran wiped a drop of coffee on his lip onto his sleeve and turned to leave the rooftop. He caught sight of the sun rising directly over a distant triangular rooftop. It was such a striking arrangement that he dared to stare straight into the light and lost himself. Unlike the circle at the bottom of his paper cup, the sun was a burning orb made of dazzling yellow light. He released a contented sigh and reflected to himself that it was the sun that brought magic into the world.

It looked like a perfect circle, but Omran knew the star was not so perfect. Unlike on his drafting table, perfect geometry didn't exist in the real world. Omran meant 'solid structure' in his native tongue. A lover of shapes, he was perfectly named.

The sun was a ball of fire, with currents and waves and explosions. Poor sun, so powerful, so central, so important, but it always being taken for granted. Composed of countless invisible objects and constantly in motion. He could almost see all the moving parts.

The rays streamed into his dark eyes and somehow gave the illusion of geometric designs dancing on his retinas. He could see circles, triangles and hexagons arranged in dazzling tessellations like he once saw in a Mosque in Isfahan. The pattern repeated infinitely, and was also reflected in a tear of pain at the corner of his eye.

Omran read somewhere that it takes light eight minutes to reach the Earth. But what most people don't know is that once produced, the light sometimes bounced around inside the layers of the sun for months before finally being released. Finally freed from a frustrating prison, the particle rushed out, gloriously, hoping to reach infinity. This is the real reason you shouldn't look at the sun. When your eye catches the light, it means that newfound freedom only lasted eight minutes instead of years or centuries.

Snapping out of his daydream, Omran looked away from the sun, blinked and let his eyes adjust again. He looked down at the street and saw the boy again, this time walking east. Again, he was pushing his shadow ahead of him. Omran jerked in place. He looked at his watch. He'd done it again! He'd stared straight into the sun all day long! Rudy was going to kill him!

Scorching fire! Okay, maybe he wasn't that mad, but Rudy was definitely angry. 'You were STARING INTO THE SUN? *That's* your excuse?'

'Rudy... I'm sorry. It doesn't happen to me often, but sometimes a certain shape, a convergence of geometry... it captivates me. And I'm lost.'

'Are you sure you're not the blond one here, Omran? Sure, you have the Arabic name, and you're a Djinn who is hundreds of years older than me, but seriously... you get distracted by shiny objects? *Really?*'

Omran cleared his throat. 'Thousands.'

Rudy was furious and ignored him. 'I looked like a fool in front of my family! You know they're not quite accepting of our marriage. Not only are they a little freaked out about the same-sex thing, but I think they're almost more upset about the interracial thing!'

'You told them about that?'

'Well, it's not something that is a secret is it? I mean, from your name to your appearance, you're obviously not Caucasian.'

'Actually, the Caucasus Mountains really aren't that far north from where I was born, Rudy.' His husband was glaring so Omran changed the subject. 'Allah created Humans, Angels and the Djinn as separate races. So I suppose you could call it interracial...'

'My family doesn't know you're a Djinn, Omran! I just meant that they're going to view you as... foreign. And you know they're sheltered. I'm not defending it, I just want to give them a chance to adjust.'

'Or perhaps you could tell them I'm... what did you call me? 'Adorably exotic' I think you said when we met.'

Rudy was finally relaxing again. He smiled. 'Don't act like I haven't said that hundreds of times.'

Omran smiled back and they kissed. 'Thousands.' He pulled Rudy down onto the couch, his blond hair, golden and young, like the rays of the sun.

Rudy pulled back. 'You said thousands.'

'Yes, I am pretty sure in the past two and a half years you've said that at least...'

'No no no. Not now. Earlier. You said thousands. *Thousands of years?*' Rudy jumped up and looked out at the street, upset.

Omran sighed: The joys of inter-whatever relationships.

Rudy swore loudly and pulled the curtains shut. 'The neighbor! I didn't tell you what happened this morning! He came over and talked to me. He said he knows...'

Omran raised an eyebrow. 'Knows what? Maybe it was the rainbow flag bumper sticker on your car that gave it away?'

'No! I think he knows... what you are.' Rudy was annoyed when his husband just laughed and threw himself into a reclining position on the couch.

'Impossible. Most people, if they see it...' Omran clapped his hands and his coffee cup floated across the room to him. '...just instantly forget that they saw it.'

'Stop that! If you want something, let me know, I'll grab it for you.'

'Oh really? Grab... anything?' Omran raised an eyebrow.

Rudy grinned. 'Of course.'

'Grab me the remote then, I want to show you something.' Rudy rolled his eyes and plopped back down onto the couch. 'Why isn't this working?'

'That's the TV remote, the DVR remote is over there. We need a universal remote.'

Omran hit the side of the TV remote. It started controlling the DVR. 'Now we have one.'

Rudy reclined and rested his head on Omran's leg. 'Stop that. What are you showing me anyway? I think we're caught up on *Dexter*.'

'This show on one of the Spanish language channels. Telemundo or Mun2 or one of those. Whichever network channel 41 is.'

At the beginning of the recording was a commercial for a 'magic' girdle which made both of them chuckle. Omran hit a button on the remote which changed all the dialog from Spanish to English. Rudy was sure this wasn't a feature of the DVR.

An old black and white cartoon started. A beautiful latina witch flew onto the screen, across the sky and landed near the doors to an orphanage. Stepping behind a cactus, she emerged from the other side as a modest light-haired beauty. The title 'Bruja Ha Ha' appeared, and somehow Rudy knew Bruja meant 'Witch'. He laughed. 'Is this from the Sixties?' Omran hushed him.

The bell from the steeple fell down, trapping a nosy disapproving nun in a giant cloud of dust. A caricature of a strange man with giant glittery glasses appeared in the cloud and winked theatrically. The words 'with Jorge Zumbido as Tio Jorge!' floated below the cartoon head.

As the live action of the sitcom began, Omran explained. 'This show, it's like us. A couple, one supernatural, one not!

There's even a nosy troublemaker always... well, making trouble.'

'Honey, I know pop culture isn't always your strong point... and thanks for buying me the Foals album by the way, that was an example of you doing good... but there are a lot of shows like this on TV. *Bewitched, I Dream of Jeanie, The Ghost and Mrs. Muir...* You didn't have to go to these extremes to show me this one. And unfortunately, none of these shows were gay. Well, except for the second Darrin. And Paul Lynde. Oh, and Charles Nelson Reilly.'

Omran was annoyed. He thought he'd discovered something unique. 'It doesn't matter. My point was that cultures are always clashing, but love finds a way. Everything ends up being fine in the end.'

Rudy turned his head and looked up into Omran's dark eyes. 'Honey, you know things don't always work out that way in the end. If these characters stepped out of the TV and found themselves in the real world, it would be quite different.'

A loud voice rang out from the flatscreen. 'Stepping out of the TV? That sounds worth trying!' The couple's heads both snapped forward just in time to see the man with the giant glasses push his way out of the screen and fall to the floor. As he dusted himself off, he transitioned from black and white into color. 'Damn wall-mounted flat-screens. They're great for crawling through, but awful for making a graceful entrance. Very roomy, but much too high!'

Before Rudy realized it, Omran was on his feet and decked out in full Djinn mode. He'd only seen him like this a few times, turban, earrings, giant sword, the whole act. Despite the presence of a frightening intruder, Rudy found it quite sexy.

Omran pinned the invader against the wall, knocking a picture of the dog to the floor. The sword pressed into the throat of 'Uncle Jorge'. 'Who are you, what are you and what are you doing here?'

The chubby and frankly somewhat queeny Mexican man laughed. 'Omran! Mijo! I mean, my boy, don't you recognize your uncle?'

Omran stared him up and down. 'You are not Uncle Jorge. He's fictional. Nor is he my uncle.'

'No, I'm not Jorge. I just look like him. Look closer. I *am* your uncle.'

Omran's nostrils flared and Rudy swore he saw licks of flame around him. Suddenly he started laughing. 'Uncle Haydar?' He hugged the man warmly, kissing him on both cheeks.

Omran turned. 'Rudy, meet my Uncle Haydar. Uncle, meet my husband!'

His eyebrows raised. 'Husband?   My, things have changed.'

Rudy composed himself. 'Gaydar?'

'Haydar, my nephew-in-law. Haydar. It means lion.' The man let out a fake roar, miming giant paws and gave Rudy a big bear hug.

'Nice to meet you, Haydar, but why do you look like this? Why don't you appear as your real self?'

Haydar turned and looked Omran up and down. 'Oh, I thought we weren't doing real forms today.   Perhaps your husband will join me?' Rudy looked confused.

Omran quickly came forward and hurried Haydar into the dinning room. 'You can wear whatever form you wish, Uncle, I'm just glad to have someone from the family visiting us in our home. Let me offer you hospitality. Rudy, would you get us some of the tea I just made from the kitchen?'

'When did you make tea?'

He snapped his fingers. 'Just now. Thanks honey.'

As soon as Rudy left the room, Omran snapped his fingers and the visage of Jorge Zumbido disappeared leaving an older Middle Eastern man wearing a Nehru jacket in his place.

Haydar looked at his reflection in a spoon. 'My, that's probably more what he expects from your uncle, isn't it. Very distinguished, although I'm not sure I should be so gray.

Maybe just a little salt and pepper.' He grabbed the salt and pepper shakers, shook some of each into his hands. He rubbed them together vigorously. He then clapped his hands together with a large thundercrack and a poof of smoke. He looked in the spoon again. Most, but not all of the gray hair had disappeared. 'Much better. Old enough to be respected, but not so old as to be dismissed. As for the jacket, it's not exactly right is it, it's a bit... Indian?'

'Indian, Arabian, he won't know the difference. Besides, we're not in Babylon anymore, Uncle. Fashions change.'

'Change is constant. Remember Babel? The tower? That was a mess when that came crashing down.'

Keith was getting his mail and saw the kitchen light come on in the house across the street. It was the white one, doing something in front of the sink.

Throwing the mail back in the box, he hurried across the street to peek in the living room window. He could hear a loud, thick accented voice echoing from further inside the house. He heard something about 'tower' and 'crashing down'.

Peering in cautiously, Keith could see structural plans laid out on what must be Omran's desk. So it was true! But what else could it mean? The neighbors were scoping out structures to attack, assessing the weak points, no doubt – like the terrorists they were! Well, the dark one was, at least! He was now positive about his suspicions. He knew Omran's secret. Keith had to hear more.

Upon returning with the tea, Rudy was confused by the new man in the dining room. Haydar theatrically whispered to Omran, 'You'd think with their silly brief lives they'd be able to remember things better.'

Omran tutted and put his arm around Rudy. 'There's nothing silly about anyone's life, Uncle. I'm proud to share it with Rudy.'

'What do you mean brief? Haydar, Omran always dodges the question, so I'm glad you're here. How long do the Djinn live?'

Omran looked annoyed. 'I told you Rudy, nobody knows how long they have. There are no guarantees in life. And however long either of us have is how long we will be together.'

Rudy moved away from his husband. 'I have no doubt you're sincere, Omran. But sometimes I get the distinct feeling that you're downplaying how long you would have to be a widower were I to pass on.'

Haydar was sitting with his arms folded, somewhat uncomfortably. 'Nephew. Do you remember Nibal?'

'Of course I do, Uncle. The mortal woman you fell in love with. I think of her often. In fact, it was your willingness to court a mortal that opened my mind to the possibilities.'

Haydar laughed. 'Indeed. And you've surpassed me in your openness to… unique romantic situations.' He stood and put his arm on Rudy's shoulder, looking into his eyes. 'I can see you have a fine mate in this man. A man as worthy of your love as Nibal was of mine. But I have a regret in regards to Nibal. I regret I was never honest with her about our time together. We grew old together. We had children. But almost 13 centuries after promising that we would meet again, still she waits for me in the afterlife. She never knew.'

Omran came around the table and stood close to his uncle, avoiding Rudy's gaze. Haydar was still talking, much more quietly now. 'I understand you. That is why I'm the only family member that responded to your invitation. They think I've forgotten Nibal. They think I'm a carefree astral-plane hopping playboy.' The last few words came out almost as a whisper.

Rudy felt a lump in his throat and finally Omran met his eyes. They were filled with sadness.

Haydar suddenly laughed nervously and stood. 'Don't get me wrong!' he said with forced cheer. 'I have a delightful time rubbing elbows with Djinn, Witches and Warlocks at the *Mushtarie* Club. That's Jupiter to you, my dear Nephew-in-law.

The solar system is an amazing place.' It was as if the man was intentionally trying to talk so fast that he'd forget his sorrow.

'In fact, Omran you'd be astounded! Just a few decades ago I met a *Sentient* at the Mushtarie lounge! An actual *Sentient!* You must understand Rudy, the Sentients are an ancient and all but mythological race who...' Suddenly Haydar's head snapped to the left and he was alert. He whispered. 'There's someone outside.'

Rudy groaned. 'That would be our nosy neighbor. I wish he'd learn to leave us alone.'

Haydar's head flicked back to face Rudy with a wild grin. 'Be careful when you make a wish when you have two Djinn in the house!' He clapped his hands and vanished before Omran could stop him.

'Uncle, no!'

Keith could hear very little and was feeling a bit guilty and paranoid. He remembered now that Omran was an architect, and supposed that the technical drawings could be for his work. But that would be the perfect cover for a terrorist! He just couldn't shake his suspicions. However, he decided it was probably time for him to extricate himself from the shadows.

It was at that moment, things started to happen.

Through the window, Keith saw a dozen men with bushy beards in turbans rush into the room and started unrolling huge scrolls onto a table. They were all talking loudly in a guttural tongue. One of them grabbed the game Jenga from a shelf and started assembling a tower as another held a compass, calculating the angle that a toy plane should hit it. Another held models of the Titanic and the Hindenburg and angled them towards the building menacingly.

Keith was shaking. He couldn't believe it. It was his worst fears materialized before his eyes. Every paranoid thought was being confirmed! Afraid he was going to scream and be discovered, he scurried away from the house. He had to get to safety and call the authorities. He ran into the street.

Omran and Rudy rushed into the living room and saw 15 duplicates of Uncle Haydar in stereotypical terrorist costumes.

'Uncle! What have you done?'

The laughter of all fifteen Haydars was silenced by the sound of screeching tires in the street outside. All 30 eyes turned and looked out the window in horror as one of them accidentally knocked over the Jenga tower. 'Oops.'

Rudy and Omran hurried outside. A minivan was stopped in the street with the driver's side door wide open. The keys were still in the ignition, so the vehicle produced an incessant electronic dinging. A woman stood over Keith, hysterical. She was on her phone, trying to talk to 911. Rudy helped her to sit down and took the phone from her to talk to the emergency operator.

Omran checked Keith who had crumpled into a surprisingly small shape on the ground where he'd been hit. When Rudy was done on the phone, he hurried to his husband's side.

'Rudy, he's dead.' Rudy looked down at Keith's lumpy form and then over to the silhouette of Uncle Haydar still standing in shock in front of the living room window.

The dinging suddenly stopped. In fact, Rudy looked around to see everything had stopped. He realized Omran had paused time.

'You can use your powers to heal him, right? Like the time I burnt myself right after we first met!'

Omran shook his head. 'No, I can't.'

'Why are you always so stubborn? Why don't you want to use your powers for major things? I know you told me to just accept it that you'll do little things on occasion, but you won't make us millionaires or anything. But why not?'

'Rudy. Fine. I'll tell you. I had another mortal lover once. Someone I loved as much as... as I love you. One afternoon, I got distracted. I noticed the galaxy spinning. I stopped and watched it turn the smallest fraction of a turn.

'That's a weakness of my people. We're immortal. We can observe the universe on a scale you can only dream about.

I'd spent a tiny sliver of my time observing a motion. A shape. And in that fingersnap, my lover had grown old and died. This was back in the days when mortal men lived several hundreds years longer than they do now, but it was over just as quickly. He died alone and lonely, never knowing what had happened to me or why I'd abandoned him.'

Rudy didn't know what to say but put his arms around Omran. He knew both of them had relationships before each other, but to learn about such a tragic loss was shocking. 'Why didn't you use your powers? Go back in time?'

'Rudy, I'm thousands of years old. I'll live for many tens of thousands years or more. Instant gratification is completely meaningless. If you can have something without fear of ever losing it, it's worthless. Even though I could have gone back, even though I could go back now... if I did, it would mean I would eventually grow tired of it. Knowing I could never lose someone would make me not care if I lost them or not.'

Rudy lifted Omran's chin gently. Then he slapped him across the face, hard. 'Oh really. Is that why you're able to commit to marriage with a mortal? Because you know that it'll be over soon enough? Because eventually my dog-years will be up, like Keith here? Would you have married me if I was immortal?'

Omran refused to look at him and Rudy raised his hand

to slap him again. But he felt a hand holding him back. Haydar was standing next to him.

'Nephew-in-law. Don't be angry with your husband who loves you very much. Be angry with me. My foolishness caused this man to die. And it isn't in my power to fix it. Life and death is in the hands of Allah.'

The trio stood there silently until Haydar's bowed head abruptly jerked up.. 'Wait. There is a way.'

Omran shook his head. 'No. I know what you are thinking. This was an accident, we aren't responsible.'

Haydar took a deep breath. 'Life can't be granted. He can be brought back to life with the sacrifice of the mortality of another.'

Rudy let that sink in. 'So, one of us can die in his place. One of us can die so this ignorant paranoid fearmonger can live! Wonderful!'

Haydar clenched his teeth. 'Regardless of the kind of man he was, that man has died because of me.'

Omran stood and held his husband's hands in his own. 'It's not that simple, Rudy. The sacrifice of mortality means exactly that. Giving up mortality. A Djinn cannot grant this because a Djinn is not mortal.'

Haydar bit the end of his thumb. 'No, but a Djinn can effect a trade. Trade his immortality for mortality.'

'Uncle, restoring this fool to life would make him immortal and powerful. Not only would you take his place in death, but you'd have made things ten times as bad.'

Haydar had a glazed look in his eyes that quickly vanished. 'That's not what I intend. You didn't let me finish. I can trade, then... trade again. Trade first with the living, then... with the dead.' Rudy was confused why the two men were now looking at him, but quickly realized what Haydar had in mind. He looked from Omran's eyes to Haydar's. In unison the three of them looked down to Keith's motionless body.

Omran opened his mouth to object, but Haydar silenced him. 'I was careless and caused this man's death. Earlier I called them 'silly brief lives'. But all lives are precious. And for years I have been irresponsible. Futile years I have spent easily because I didn't care about their passing.' He unbuttoned his Nehru jacket and relaxed. He looked exhausted. 'I look at myself and see pointless, wasted years. I look at you two and see many fulfilling years together ahead of you. Years that could be centuries, if you want them.'

Rudy stared into his husband's face. The silence was deafening. Omran spoke again. 'I am not so different to Keith. It was my fear and paranoia speaking. I love you and want to be with you as long as I can. Longer than just a few dog years. But this is a big change that can't be undone.'

Haydar sighed and smiled grimly. He stood between the two men like a minister, which was highly appropriate for that moment. 'You are sure about this? Both of you?' The husbands had tears in their eyes. They hadn't even discussed it, but they knew. They both smiled and nodded.

Rudy watched as Haydar gathered one of Omran's tears with a finger. Haydar then touched Rudy's cheek and it felt familiar to Rudy, comforting. A tear trickled down and came to rest on Haydar's finger like a robin landing on a branch.

Haydar turned, his hands wet with the tears of lovers. He looked down at the injured man and felt shame and regret. The man was disgusting and bigoted, but it was fear and ignorance that made him that way. He still deserved life. Haydar let a love for the man build in him. Not a love like Rudy and Omran shared, but a love for one's fellow man, be they Human or Djinn, male or female, American or Iraqi or Babylonian. Christian, Jewish or Muslim.

All those barriers that could block love were gone and Haydar released his regret for causing the loss of this man's life in the form of tears. Not a shower or a torrent, but tears that gradually built up one by one until reaching a critical mass and slowly running down his face, dripping from his chin, onto his hands, mixing with the tears of the lovers. 'Nibal, my love...' A few tears finally fell down onto the still figure on the ground.

There was no flash of light or celestial song, but it was done. Time started again. The car door was dinging and vehicles could be heard in the distance. Omran saw the figure standing in front of him turn around in surprise. It was Keith, standing exactly where his uncle had been. Haydar lay at his feet, dead.

It was morning. It had been a few weeks and Rudy didn't feel any different about waking up and getting ready for work even though he was now a Djinn. Between him and Haydar, they had restored Keith's life. Keith was now alive, like any mortal, and Rudy was adjusting to being immortal. Haydar was now with Nibal. It took some shuffling, but the balance had been kept.

Keith was just as difficult as ever, but fortunately didn't remember anything of the incident. Rudy made a point to interact with him and be civil even though it was difficult. He was determined to make a change in the man and expand his mind and that would never happen if he avoided him. Love thy neighbor.

Omran was just getting out of the shower and was toweling off. Rudy cleared his throat. 'I should find it extremely exciting that you're parading around nude in front of me, but I can only think about how I have horrible breath and I need coffee. Then I'll have coffee breath. Is this the death of romance in our marriage?'

He leaned down and gave Rudy a smooch. 'I will still kiss you good morning no matter what kind of breath you have.'

'How will you feel in one hundred years? Or two hundred? Will there still be a fire between us?'

'That's a worry every couple has on some level. Granted, on a different scale. Besides, speaking of fire – now that you're a Djinn, there's something you should know.' Omran dropped his towel.

Rudy raised an eyebrow. 'Oh? What's that?'

'Uncle Haydar hinted at it that night. Our true forms.' Omran clapped and started to radiate heat. He burned bright red, an aura of flames all around him. 'The Djinn. We are beings of smokeless fire.'

Rudy took a deep breath and experimentally clapped. When nothing happened, Omran reached out a hand. 'Let me show you.' At his husband's touch, Rudy's skin burned an intense sapphire color and he took a moment to adjust to the sensation.

They kissed deeply and passionately. Omran ran his hands through Rudy's hair and watched the red flames mix with the blue. 'Rudy, I'm scared that it won't last. Scared because I want it to. Scared...'

'Omran. Hush. Everyone's scared. And being scared does some ugly things to a person. That's why we have each other as long as it lasts. It could be a dog year or a galactic twirl. Relax.'

Omran grinned. 'I'd like to take a twirl with you.'

'Dancing? Here and now?'

'I meant a galactic twirl. But here and now is a nice place to be with you.' They kissed gently. 'But we have to get to work and I think our being on fire is freaking out the dog.'

The Tain of the Mirror

Jonathan Kemp

I watch you.

You pull away from the ornate looking-glass, leaving a condensation-flower centred by the sticky imprint of your lips. You turn to me and smile. It is a smile I can only return painfully, my face still swollen, my split lip stinging. My right eye is a tender purple and ink blue mound, big as an egg, from your fist. I cannot recall now why we fought. I only remember wanting to die.

I have never hated anyone as much as I did you, then. I've never loved anyone as much as I do you, now.

You are by my side, running a cautious hand through my hair, as if handling a small, fragile bird.

'Your hair', you murmur, 'so black – black as a raven.'

'Black as sin', I say.

The first night floats back to me. You big and gentle, smiling like a beacon, pleading with me to let you take me home, saying I was the most beautiful man you'd ever laid eyes on. I laughed, unimpressed. But I was lonely, and more than a little drunk. I said I don't normally do this sort of thing. You didn't believe me. Still don't.

Your kiss. So brutal. A forewarning – if only I'd noticed – of the violence to come. This room of yours. My prison. (I haven't left it since that first night.) I know it so well. As well as I know your body. Intimate with its every line, every contour, every corner, every inch. Its rhythms. Its shadows.

The charred aroma of candles, always.

'I hate artificial light', you said as we arrived here that first night, setting an orangey-blue match flame to the wicks of a forest of tall, snow white candles till the room ignited, casting dancing veils of shadow across the walls, like a genie clouding from a lamp.

A bulbous vase of Arum lilies stands proudly by the side of the mirror, exhaling its heavy scent. As you stand there gazing at yourself, I am reminded of that scene in Cocteau's *Orphée* where Orpheus enters a door-sized mirror, stepping through its liquid surface and disappearing into the underworld. You too would enter that mirror if you could, Narcissus of the night. Slowly we undress, facing one another, and as we remove the same garments simultaneously, we become the reflection of each other. Then, just as I am anticipating a kiss or a touch, you turn and face the mirror.

I watch you lick your ochre reflection, your glassy double, then walk over to a record player and place the stylus onto the record that is already on the turntable. The sound of crackling, like logs on a fire, fills the room temporarily, before the first, slow purr of a cello sounds. Bach. You begin to dance with your reflection, not taking your eyes from it, and for a second I wonder what my role is here. I am your audience. I move over to the bed and sit down. The candle flames curtsy and bow in deference to your wild dervishing. Your dancing partner in the glass keeps perfect time, mirroring your every move. And shadows flit and skip across the walls and ceiling, like girls around a Maypole. I watch you dip and spin to the staccato music as it crashes in wave after wave; until, finally, as the music stops, you come in a noisy crescendo of hot wax against the glass. Then you fall to the floor, all passion spent, panting like a wolf.

I can hear the rapid thud of your heart from here.

You only wanted me here as voyeur. You never even noticed my desires; my pleasure is secondary to yours, something I should assuage myself by watching you curl a hand around your ardent cock and immerse yourself in that solitary act, occupying yourself with your own flesh, your own desires. We never touched. Never touch. I soon became uncomfortably ashamed of my own desires till they subsided altogether. Now it never occurs to me to desire. Just watch, as you pose and dance. Watch as your sperm globs onto the glass and runs down in pearly clots. The music, something classical. Often opera. Or sometimes, the lilting blues of Billie Holiday. A threnody of woe and thwarted love.

'It's strange', you said once, to your reflection, to the room, perhaps to me, 'that there are parts of our bodies that we never see. I know every inch of mine.' And you proceeded to inspect your perineum with obscene, methodical, scientific interest, probing and stretching your flesh, pinching your scrotum till it blanched, then letting go, watching in awe as the fleshy pinkness returned. Fascinated by your own body, but not mine; never mine. My body held no interest for you. The richest regions of my dark continent contain no precious ores or metals you wish to mine, no unknown treasures to exhume and appropriate. I was left feeling freakish and grotesque, out of place, which is what you desired all along, I suspect. My attraction lay, did it not, in my mystery, your desire to obliterate my self. What can I do but wonder what I have done to deserve so little, wonder why there is no love, and if I even warrant any, my expectations tatty and undefined.

I cannot recall when or why the fights began. I remember your hard fists smashing into everything, crunching into my face. At first, I tried to fight back, beating you with inept fists. Then I cried, 'Go on, then! Fucking kill me!' until I collapsed from sheer exhaustion, shuddering in your arms.

I slept, awaking to the sound of your voice crooning my name. I thought it was a song at first. My crusted eyes groped for focus.

In your hand, a flower.

Why did I stay?

That question is a church bell tolling lugubriously inside my head, dull, heavy and repetitive. I do not know, I do not know. Love, I suppose. Will that suffice? Does it ever?

The tenderness after the violence, the pleading kisses, like the relief at the end of pain. Your tears, your kisses, your remorse. I'm not sure I could live without them.

Sometimes I think that I invented you; created you in a wild fantasy one dull night to amuse myself. But then you got too big for your boots and came stomping into reality like Frankenstein's monster and crushed the very life breath out of me like a ham-fisted accordion playr.

Or did you create me, the ultimate voyeur before whom to perform your Narcissus dance? Was it me who slipped the noose of unreality and became the dream made flesh, maddening with my cravings for love?

I no longer know. Either way, your need to be adored fed and shaped my need to adore. Like a mathematical equation, our balance was absolute. Until, that is, the inevitable moment arrived when your violence outweighed my adoration, and the long unraveling of my love began.

And so here you are, before me, gripping your hard cock and sighing, catching your breath as the sexual tension in your body gathers momentum. You flex the bicep of your free arm, lost in your reflected beauty. Bored, I look away, and you notice, barking the single angry word, 'WATCH!' I observe with indifference as your sticky dart hits the glass like so many times before.

You walk towards me, glistening with orange, candle-flamed sweat, and climb into the bed beside me; this bed raised like a catafalque, the white sheets shrouding me like cerecloth. Your arms encircle my numb body. Your hot breath tickles the nape of my neck as your lips sculpt a kiss, and this one act of tenderness keeps me manacled to you with chains no less imprisoning for their invisibility. I plummet into a restless sleep from which I know I must, sadly, awaken, and I hate myself. I hate you. I hate these tears. I hate your kiss, for it annihilates me and resurrects me as if I were Lazarus, my purulent, blue-bottled stench cocooning me in a cell of stagnant unfreedom. The huge, yellowy black patch of tender flesh from my bruised shoulder to my waist aches far less than my withered heart.

We stagger like drunkards between tenderness and torture, back and forth without end, while I close my eyes and wish myself away from here, desperate for freedom yet scared to break free.

I am still unsure whether it was I who caused your death. All I know is that minutes before it happened I had been willing it, and perhaps my thoughts invoked some vengeful, telekinetic demon to enact for me so meticulously your sublime decapitation.

There you were: one second, spinning vertiginously, like a top, the next, you faltered, unbalanced enough to send you careering headlong through the looking-glass. This was no cunning pool of water posing as a mirror. This was the real thing, brittle and murderous. Your beautiful head crashed like a cannonball into the centre of the mirror, bringing the full weight of the top half guillotining down through the soft stalk of your slender neck. Easy as an oar blade cutting water. The florid wooden frame remains there, magnificently displaying the entire bloody scene.

And the mess; blood everywhere.

I never imagined so much blood in you. It decorates the walls in great promontories of red, mapping the geography of your destruction. There is a strange beauty in this image before me that far outweighs my grief. I am alarmingly calm. This tranquility both surprises and scares me. After all, had I not desired this for longer than I cared to remember? Pictured it. Willed it. Felt intoxicated with its rich liqueur. (Dreams really can come true!) I only murdered you in thought, though, not deed. My hands remain stain-free, my conscience clean of the grime of guilt. Death by misadventure. The kind of sticky end expected of those foolish enough to dance like a dervish before full-length mirrors.

And what of me now? The liberated me, unmanacled and eager to resume a life of feigned normality? But what is normality now if not this strangulating dependence upon another, this irrational fear of freedom and independence?

My future is a pathway which snakes itself into the ominous curled figure of a question-mark, devil-black and grinning.

First I must escape this incarcerating room. Your bloodied, headless corpse is beginning to stink, the buzz of flies incessant, like amplified static. The meaty stench of you makes me retch. Your head, once detached from your body, rolled next to the vase of lilies and sits there now, on the stumpy plinth of your bloody neck, grimacing, manic-eyed, a sinister mouth twist that unnervingly resembles a smile. (Was it my imagination, or did your eyes really meet mine with a pitiful plea as your severed head rocked into place?)

All the candles have long since guttered out; the lilies long since dead.

I stand up and cautiously tiptoe through the sparkling minefield of mirror shards starring the floorboards. In a slice of broken mirror propped up against the wall, I catch my own pale, naked reflection, and I see it in a new, invigorating light.

That jagged blade of silver-tained glass throws back a vision I have never seen before. I am beautiful. I start to dance, timidly at first, but soon I am giddy, laughing like a child, taking no heed of the vicious splinters, sharp as shark's teeth underfoot. Turning, I throw a look over my shoulder and catch my reflection again, and for the first time in I don't know how long, I smile, and the spectral reflection smiles too, dazzlingly.

Soul Man

Joseph Lidster

I've never kept a diary or blog before. I've never really seen the point. They've always struck me as a bit introspective and self-indulgent. I know what I've done and I know what I think about so why write it down? I mean, it's like Twitter. Who are you meant to be talking to? And, to be honest, after the things— no. Not things. It's not just things. They're deaths. And why would I want to dwell on them?

Okay, that was a crap opening. Sorry about that. I'm just not used to doing this whole thinking about things thing. And I certainly don't like to think about you. About death. Who would?

You know that thing people say about staring death in the face? They say it when they've had cancer or been in a car accident or something. Well, I've done that but I mean it the other way. I've stared death in the face because I've seen the bodies. I had to look at the pictures when the police interviewed me. As you know, they soon realised it wasn't me but, of course, they still don't know who the killer was. They still don't know it was you.

Yeah. I know. I know it was you. I think I always knew from that first moment I saw you at the Prom. I wonder why you did it? I mean, I sort of know why you did it. I know the bland technical reasons behind it but I wonder if even you know what drove you to it. I wonder if you even know *what* you are.

And the thing is, I know you're going to do it again and I know that, one day, you'll do it to me. It's funny, in a way, that I feel pretty calm about that. So much of life is strange and scary and you don't know what's going to happen. People wake up and then they die. Or they die in their sleep. Or they get drunk and find a boy or a girl. Or they have a tuft of hair that sticks up no matter how much product they put on it. Every day, it's different. We don't know what's going to happen. We've not got control, not really. And knowing, actually knowing, that one day you'll end my life, and knowing that it'll happen soon because I'm not going to fight it anymore, knowing all that... I don't know. It just makes everything simple. Clean. Pre-destined. I've accepted it. Soon, it'll all be someone else's problem.

And I guess, as much as it's for you, this is for that someone else. I want them to know what I discovered. I want them to know about me. The bloke who's writing this knowing full well it'll mean he'll die soon. I want to feel that I've done something good, that I've achieved something. Because we're not all like you. We're not all dark and wrong.

So, yeah, this isn't just a diary. It's an autobiography, I guess. It's about me. It's about the town I grew up in – that's Millingdale in Kent. It's about James the cokehead football player, Kym his beautiful anorexic girlfriend and the others. Because I know there are others, I just don't know their names. And it's about who killed them. It's about you.

So, right. Well, obviously you know my name. I was born on July 13th 1991. Dad was a teacher and a bastard. Mum was nondescript and worked in a garden centre. Dad left when I was four. He'd been sleeping with the deputy head and at least two of his pupils. That left me and Mum. She worked hard to make sure I had everything I wanted. Of course, my clothes were hand-me-downs and everyone knew about my Dad so I wasn't exactly Mr Popular. I mean, in London, there I'm my real self. All that doubt and loneliness pushed down. I'm me. Life and soul. Always there with a tray of shots and a comedy pratfall. But back then, in that tiny, incestuous, beautiful little town, I was nobody.

There was this time when I lost my trainers. It was after swimming and I was 11 or 12 and I reckon someone must have hidden them or something. Mr Branning wouldn't let anyone leave until we'd all traipsed to lost property. He probably thought he was doing the right thing. Showing all the kids that bullying was A Bad Thing. So there I was. And there, in lost property, were my trainers. And there they all were. My classmates. All watching as Mr Branning picked up one of the trainers and looked inside to find, written in biro, someone else's name. He looked confused for a second, wondering out loud why my trainers seemed to belong to someone else and, I think every single child in that room worked it out before he did. To give him credit, he quickly tried to cover up his mistake and, blushing, handed them over to me. But every child there knew. Every one of us knew that my mum was poor because my dad had slept with schoolchildren and that I was wearing someone else's shoes.

God, that sounds a bit grim when I write it down. But yeah, that was probably the turning point. Up until then, I'd had a couple of mates. Shaun was fat and Fiona had a hole in her heart but after the trainer thing, even they started to avoid me. I wasn't bullied so much as ignored. People simply didn't talk to me. It was like I spent my entire childhood as this invisible ghost. Oh God, sorry. See this is why I've never understood diaries. It's all just so ridiculously emo. Because things weren't that bad really. And, you know, I came out of it all right. I'm a recruitment consultant in London now. Got myself a decent haircut and my own pair of shoes. Loads of kids were bullied or ignored or poor, so I'm no different from anyone else really. And yeah, life now is pretty good.

Well, it was. Until I realised the truth about you. About the creature.

But first, Millingdale. We'll come to *you* later. Millingdale's the kind of town that people describe as picturesque. Because it is. It's on the sea and it's lovely and there are Old Worlde Tea Shops and the pub has a real log fire and those brass things that I think come from horses or something. There's not a building in Millingdale that doesn't have deliberately exposed varnished beams. I've just taken my flatmate there, actually. I didn't want to go back but you know, you have to. Mum wanted to meet her and she doesn't like London. She's scared of terrorists and pigeons.

'It looks lovely!' That's what Laurie said when we arrived. 'Picturesque!' But I said to her, I said, how behind those lovely cottages, with their polished wooden floors and Venetian blinds, were the housing estates. Hidden out of view. Kept secret from the old-women-out-for-a-drive and the lost-German-hikers. And behind the Olde Worlde Tea Shops were the chippies and the off-licenses. And I told her about the secrets. All those talked-about secrets. Mrs Cartwright's son in prison. Lizzie Bristow's special friendship with her sister-in-law. The Bonfire Night/post office incident.

And the murder. I couldn't *not* tell her about the murder. It was, let's be honest, the biggest thing that had happened there. James. The football player. 16 years old. Bashed over the head with a brick and then strangled to death. For once, the Millingdale Post was given the glorious gift of a headline that wasn't about a missing cat or local planning dispute.

James Unsworth. He was the captain of the football team. He was tall, blonde, fit, a bit of a dick. He was perfect. A walking cliché. I'm sure, you know, he had hidden depths but me, the invisible ghost, never got chance to discover them. Part of me wishes I had. Maybe if I'd spoken to him or discovered his secret passion for stamp-collecting or what music he was into, maybe it wouldn't have happened. I think everyone feels guilty when someone dies. Especially in a town like Millingdale. I mean, I'm pretty certain I couldn't have stopped you killing him but I just felt guilty for not really knowing this guy I'd grown up with. But for me, James was a thing not a person. Frankly, he was walking porn. An object of desire, not a real human being at all.

He'd been going out with Kym for a couple of years. I'm not sure they had anything in common really. They were just the beautiful people. The football captain and the star of the drama society. With perfect bodies and perfect teeth. Mr and Mrs Perfect.

It was the night of the school prom. We'd finished our GCSEs and it was time to say goodbye. Some were going to stay on and do A-levels. Some, like me, who'd spent the previous couple of years discovering the joyous oblivion of cider, well... I didn't know what I was going to do. Mum had got me a summer job at the garden centre but after that, I didn't know.

The prom was everything you expected it to be. The beautiful people looked beautiful. The cliques hugged each other and promised to stay in touch. The teachers got discreetly drunk. So many smiling faces. But behind it all, you could sense the fear. The fear of the unknown. Dancing couples promising their eternal love but knowing, after that night, that they'd drift apart as one went to college and the other went to work for their parents. And, there, in the middle of it all, were James and Kym. Owning the dance floor as they'd owned school for the last few years. We all orbited them and they loved it. Actually, it was probably good he died that night. Before he got fat and became a nobody. The beautiful man. The beautiful object. The centre of attention. Perfect body and perfect teeth.

And then there was you. I could see you on the other side of the room. I didn't know who you were but you looked familiar. I just assumed you were some other kid from school.

Another one who'd looked through me as you'd passed me in the corridor. But you weren't looking through me that night. You were looking at me as I watched James. And you were smiling. I saw that when I glanced back at you. You smiling. And you didn't have perfect teeth. Your teeth were black.

I just had a thought. Did you come from the sea? I don't suppose you'd tell me even if you knew yourself.

I don't remember much else from the Prom. I got absolutely shitfaced on some cheap rum I'd smuggled in. Apparently, Mr Branning, possibly still feeling guilty for exposing me all those years before, put me in a taxi which he paid for. I remember one thing and one thing only. Someone, possibly Mr Branning or my mum when she put me to bed, muttering about what a shame it was. And I knew they were talking about me. Hashtag emo.

The following morning, I was sacked from the garden centre for throwing up in an ornamental water feature. And as I limped home, tears in my eyes from the hangover, I realised that people were whispering. The whole town was whispering. *Well, I heard Mary talking about it in Costcutter and she says it was up on Tracey Bridge.* And *Ooh, Jane just heard from Sarah at the taxi rank that it was definitely James Unsworth.* And then *Murdered! He was definitely murdered!*

And yeah. James had been murdered. Apparently, he'd argued with Kym at the Prom because he'd been seen with someone else. He'd got drunk and stormed off. But he'd never made it home. He'd been found, the following morning, by some hiking Norwegians on the bridge that led out of town. He had a fractured skull that hadn't killed him and a crushed windpipe that had.

We were all called in to see the police. In a town that size it's easier just to treat everyone as a suspect. Someone had told them that they'd seen me staring at James so I was very much under suspicion but once Mr Branning and the taxi driver and my mum had explained just how drunk I'd been, it was clear that I couldn't have done it. I didn't tell them about you. About your black teeth smiling at me. I wish I had. It might have saved the others. But how could I? I didn't know what you were. A demon? Who'd have believed me?

The police never found out who did it. Over the next few months, the town would gasp in delighted shock as someone would be arrested and they'd shake their heads in delighted disbelief as that someone would then be released due to a lack of evidence. And eventually, the murder became just another bit of local history. Kym, like many of us, moved away but not before giving the performance of her life at James's funeral. Seriously, it was Oscar-worthy. A skirt just short enough to show off her matchstick legs without appearing slutty. And the tears, the beautiful tears that never seemed to smudge her make-up. I'm sure she was genuinely upset but that didn't mean she couldn't play up for her audience.

I didn't go to the funeral. I thought it'd be a bit weird. I mean, I didn't really know him. And I didn't want to think of his body in the coffin. I mean, what if I'd got an erection at the funeral? A stiffy thinking about a stiff! Hashtag awkward.

And so, like Kym, I moved away from Millingdale. She went off to some drama academy and became mildly renowned for sleeping with another footballer. This one was famous so she'd gone up in the world. I went to London to seek my fortune. Well, not so much that as to reinvent myself. By then, of course, I knew I was gay, which wasn't something the people in Millingdale were too keen on. Like ethnic minorities and recycling, gays were *fine*. Just, well, you know, Millingdale is *very* picturesque and historical and just not, you know, we don't have a problem with it, it's just, you know, it's the sort of thing they do, you know, in that there London. Hashtag embarrassedmumble.

***

But London? Oh, in that there London I thrived! You know that clip they always show on telly when they're talking about the 1960s? That black-and-white woman trotting down Carnaby Street grinning along to whatever Beatles track the producers can afford? That's London. Cheap, nasty, superficial but fucking brilliant. Because nobody cares who that black-and-white woman is. She's just a thing, a person. Another grinning person walking through the crowds. And yeah, obviously, there are homeless people and scary people and late trains and stuff but, for the most part it's just millions and millions of faceless, black-and-white people pushing through each other, shopping and drinking and shagging. They don't care about each other and they most certainly didn't care about me, their latest fellow citizen. It was so bloody refreshing. After years of everyone knowing who I was because of my Dad and the trainers and everything, suddenly I was in a place where nobody knew me. I could do anything I wanted. So I went shopping and bought some decent clothes and got myself a decent hairstyle. And I joined a gym and I took up smoking. And I became someone new. No, not someone new. Me. The me I've always been. And I nearly forgot about you. The demon I'd seen on the night of the murder. Looking at me through the deluded, dancing couples and grinning.

I suppose I should have felt bad about not reporting you. James had had his life taken away and I was living it up in that there London. But in London, you live for the moment. You don't think about what was or what's still to come. You rush onto that Tube train, you rush through your day at work, you rush into that bar, you rush into bed with an unsuitable man. There's no time to think. No time to dwell. You know, I bet there aren't many Londoners who keep diaries. And yes, I know there's Samuel Pepys but I'm not counting him because he lived in the past and he's dead.

I joined a temping agency where they seem surprised that I could string a sentence together. They got me a job at this recruitment consultancy. Bit of filing, data input that kind of thing. Nothing that involved thinking or anything. But I was good and I liked it there and they liked me so they took me on and gave me a pay-rise and a career. I actually had money in the bank! And I loved it. I loved how it was this beautiful rush of workmates and leaving cards and maternity leaves and cigarette breaks and nights out and no thinking. No real thinking. No real friendships. Oh, we'd stay in touch on Facebook but it was all so casual. People would join then they'd leave. Students, travellers, temps. Yeah, that's it. Temps. It was all so temporary. A permanent state of being temporary. Oh, I can't decide whether that's profound or makes me sound like a wanker? Ah, sod it. I might be dying after I write this so I don't care how I sound. I might start making up words as well.

Just because I can. If there's one thing you've given me, it's a lack of careability about spellingandgrammar because you're going to kill me and who's whose whoooooooois going to mark this? Mr Branning? The old fucker's dead. Well, they think he's dead. He disappeared last Boxing Day. Went out to get the papers and never came back. I wonder if that was you, as well?

Actually, now I do just sound stupid. And paranoid. Okay, on with the story.

Laurie Hooper. Fellow recruitment consultant. Fat girl. One of those girls about who people would say 'oh, but she's got a great personality' if she had one. The most you could say about her was that she was... fine. Harmless. Mostly harmless. Mostly blubber. She needed a flatmate and I needed a flatmate so we moved in together and watched DVD boxsets of *The West Wing* so we could admire the *wonderful clever* dialogue without actually having to have a dialogue ourselves. So yeah, she's fine. We get drunk. She says she wishes I was straight. I say I wish she was Tom Hardy. She gets a little too close for comfort and I make a speedy exit to my bedroom and the delights of Grindr.

Grindr. Oh, sweet Grindr. Who needs relationships when you can message someone based on the fact they've got a great set of abs? I won't go into detail about the boys of London town because my Mum might read this but yeah, there were many available. And I took advantage of that. They didn't even have to have names. Very few of them even had faces.

And so, that was my life. My temporary life of abs and fat girls and black-and-white people. And I was actually happy. And I forgot about you.

As for going back to Millingdale? I'd go home for Christmas, obviously, but for the most part I'd make up some excuse. And Mum was on Facebook and Skype so we could stay in touch that way. Never had much to say to her anyway. 'Yeah, work's fine. Yeah, Laurie's fine. Yeah, everything's fine. Everything fine there? Good. Fine. Speak to you next weekend. Yeah. Love you too.'

Funny thing that. Saying 'Love you too' I mean. Because I don't know if I did. I don't know if I've ever really loved anyone. There's never been time. I guess I never will now.

Laurie and Mum became Facebook friends and, for some reason, wanted to meet up in real life. I didn't see the point but they pestered and moaned and went on and on about it and it gave me a headache and, eventually, I just said... fine. I shouldn't have. It's not like I'd really forgotten about you. God, there were even times in London when I thought I saw you. Glimpses of you in the crowds. Your white face and black teeth. Grinning at me from behind the counter at Boots. Knocking back a cocktail in the Yard. Showing off your abs on Grindr. But it wasn't you. I was just being paranoid.

Because you'd stayed in Millingdale. And I saw you the moment I got back.

You're one of the secrets of that picturesque little town, aren't you? Do the others know about you? Do they talk about you behind my back? Do they know you killed James? Where are you from? The sea? The air? The depths of the Earth? What the fuck are you?

We stayed with my Mum which worked out well because she likes cooking and Laurie likes eating. But all I could think about was you. I'd seen you in the car mirror as I drove in. Waiting for me. I wanted to get out of the car and shout. Why me? What had I ever done? But I didn't. I ignored you. You know why? Because I was terrified that nobody else would be able to see you. Imagine that? I wasn't scared of what you'd done or what you might do, I was scared that I might be going mad.

I wasn't the only one to return to Millingdale that week. High-school queen and reality TV heroine Kym Ashman was back. The town that barely acknowledged me, worshipped her because she'd broken up some famous footballer's marriage. Like me, she'd changed her appearance. But we were different. I was the real me. The fit, funny, successful me I'd always been under the flab and fear. She looked like she was wearing a costume. So preened and pampered and pouty. I don't know who she thought she was. She looked fake.

We bumped into each other in the White Rabbit. She was catching up with her old cronies and I'd been forced to take Laurie out. Her old schoolfriends were a cackling bunch who, as they had years before, swarmed around her like flies on shit. One of them must have recognised me because they waved me over. Or maybe they fancied the new — no, real — me? Either way, I found myself leaving Laurie at the bar and crouching down next to Kym. She hadn't stood to greet me, of course. And she didn't recognise me. She hadn't got a clue who I was. I reminded her about what I'd used to look like, about the trainers, about being sick at the Prom, about the time her boyfriend had pushed me into Lake Windermere on a school trip. But no. She didn't have a fucking clue. She was interested, though, when I mentioned that I now lived in London with my boyfriend, a television producer called Julian.

Yes. I know. I don't even know why I did it. I don't know why I said I had a boyfriend or why I said he was a TV producer. I've never even met anyone called Julian. But it meant that suddenly I was Someone To Talk To. The Invisible Ghost was suddenly tangible. We talked and talked about the bars and clubs of London, getting to the point where even her loyal cronies were looking bored. Laurie, in an actual first, had pulled, so she'd gone. And it wasn't long before me and Kym realised that we couldn't go clubbing or on to some trendy party because such things simply didn't exist in picturesque Millingdale.

And so she came back to mine. Even now, I think it's odd how we never mentioned James once. We drank a lot of whisky. Hers on the rocks. Mine, much to her grating hysterical amusement, straight. And we talked about people from school and how glad we were to have escaped. And then, looking over her shoulder, I saw you.

In my house. In my bedroom. Smiling. And I knew we hadn't escaped. I knew that you'd killed James and that you'd kill us. I jumped up and screamed at you.

Yeah. You screamed like a girl.

What? I never wrote that.

No, I did. Your little black-toothed monster.

Oh. So you're here now? Why did you kill her?!

You don't know?

Because she ran? Because she screamed?

It wasn't me she was scared of. She couldn't see me.

It was you who ran outside after her! It was you who got into the car and drove after her and hit her. You killed her.

It was your car I was driving. If they link that bitch's death to your car, it's your name they'll find on their database. Just like the trainers.

What are you? Why did you kill Ja

Oh, will you shut up. God, you go on. All that moaning and self-pity and pathetic attempts at wit. Hashtag wanker. You're so weak. Why did I kill James? Why do you think someone would want to read this? To discover your banal thoughts on what life's all about or to hear me talk about the killing? What do you reckon? So yeah, I'll tell you. And you. I'd always lusted after that boy. And I wanted him. But I knew he wouldn't want me and so I took him. It's all very simple. I stopped him changing. Stopped him moving away. Stopped him just being temporary. Because that's the difference between us. You want everything to be temporary and fleeting. I want eternity.

And so, on the night of the Prom, I jumped out of my bedroom window and I saw him walking. So drunk. So angry. He didn't know who I was which made things so much easier. I comforted him. Gave him some rum and then, when he had his back to me, I hit him across the back of the head with the bottle and he fell to the ground. And then, oh then I strangled him. It was so intimate. So pure. So special. Underneath the moonlight with the sound of the river trickling by underneath us. I climbed on top of him and I put my hands around his neck. He had a big neck so it was harder than I'd anticipated. But also so much more exciting. You see, when you strangle someone, you're in complete control. It's not like when I hit that stupid bitch Kym with the car. That was quick and painless for us both. Strangling James... I was in control. I'd been dormant and invisible for so long but then? Then I was in total control. I gripped and squeezed and squeezed and saw the colour of his face change, felt his chest rising up beneath my legs as he tried to breathe. And then, I loosened my hands a bit. Watched his eyes flicker with relief. Felt his chest sink back down beneath me. But then, I squeezed again! And let go. Squeezed. And let go. I was in control of his life. Me! Insignificant little me with my black teeth and cheap haircut. I had control over just how long another person had left to live. Oh, and those beautiful blue eyes. They stared up at me, pleading, confused, scared, terrified, panicking, begging, hopeless, no hope, and that beautiful brief second when he realised he was going to die and...

..then with a final gasp off he went. He was so still. I'd given him eternity. A beautiful body for his eternal rest. After that, I cleaned myself up and I went home. It was a good night. You want to come back again?

Why? Why me?

You selfish bastard. You know I killed James and I killed Kym and all you can think about is yourself? And you reckon I'm the sick one!

Where are you from? What made you?

Oh, the secrets. And the lies. And the self-hatred. And this tiny little town surrounding you, smothering you, ignoring you. And you thought you'd escaped? You thought that by moving to London, it'd be different? This was pre-destined. You could never escape me.

Are you going to do it again?

Well, James was the first. Oh, and then Mr Branning. That was quite funny actually. I was driving past him and I stopped and offered him a lift. He forgot the golden rule about not getting into cars with strangers. Of course, he didn't know I was a stranger.

He thought you were me?

I am you.

You're not.

I am. And we'll do it again. Because it so easy to kill people. Once you've done it that one time, it just becomes part of life. Part of you. And it doesn't matter what you think but I am part of you. We all have our demons. The footballer addicted to coke. The anorexic actress. The respectable teacher with a taste for young flesh. And you? You have me. Eating into your soul and becoming your Soul.

Please. Leave me alone. I don't want to. I don't want this. Stop talking to me as if I'm something separate. I'm not your invisible ghost. I'm you.

Please.

Listen. Downstairs. Can you hear them laughing? Laurie and your Mummy. You know what they're laughing about. Mummy's telling the fat bitch all about your childhood. How sad you were. How lonely. She's telling her about the bedwetting and the trainers and what Daddy did.

Stop.

You can make them stop. They're in the kitchen. With the knives. We've never killed a fat girl before. Don't you wonder what it'll be like?

No.

Yes.

You're me.

We're me.

But we can't get caught and I've written all this down? What if someone reads it? Then we'll just have to find them. And they don't know who we are. We're just someone rushing through life. I'm just a set of abs on Grindr. A black-and-white person. I'm just me. Or perhaps they have a Soul as well. Perhaps they'll try it. The ecstasy of taking a life. Because it's the one thing in life we can all do, no matter who we are. Just put those hands, those shaking hands, around his neck and squeeze. Rev your engine. Pick up the knife. Take control.

I'm going downstairs now to stop them laughing. I might not have perfect teeth but I'm smiling.

The Case of the Incongruous Carrot
Wayne Clews

Glancing at herself in the mirror as she went to fetch the sherry, Muriel saw that she was a little more flushed than usual and that her paper hat had slipped. She paused for a moment, deciding that she rather liked the effect, giving her an appearance of jauntiness that she generally lacked.

'Muriel,' said Henrietta, lolling on the settee as usual, a cigarillo dangling from her lips, 'you're hat's skew-whiff. It makes you look like a drunken stevedore.'

'I doubt you even know what a stevedore is.'

'Something nautical, isn't it?'

'If anyone looks like a docker round here, it's you. Slouched like an old soak on the settee with that thing hanging out of your mouth.' She gave a quick tut and a shake of her head, causing her paper hat to fall to the floor.

'I don't think many dockers go in for tweed twin-sets,' was all Henrietta had to say on the matter. 'Oh, don't bother with the sherry, haven't you got any of that nice whisky left?'

'No, you polished it off last time you were here, don't you remember?'

'I can't say that I do.'

'I'm not surprised. The taxi driver was very reluctant to

take you as a fare to say the least. I think I have some gin in the pantry.'

'Well, it's doing no good sat in there is it? Bring it through.'

Muriel was relieved to escape the humid atmosphere of the sitting room. After a rather indulgent Christmas dinner and several glasses of port, she felt flustered and light-headed. She should have suggested a walk earlier, she supposed, doubting Henrietta would have even considered the idea. Now it was already dark and foggy, and there was no chance of such an outing and, besides, Henrietta was wearing typically impractical shoes. She sat down at the kitchen table, enjoying the cool and quiet of the room, glad that she had given Flossie, her maid, the day off. She couldn't cope with any of her fussing today and it was to be hoped that some rousing, implausibly Cockney knees-up of a Christmas might cheer her up. Flossie had been dour of late. Only yesterday she had said, whilst swilling her tea cup about, that there was an ill wind blowing and, gazing down at the tea leaves, added that death was stalking the streets.

'I think we can safely say that death is always stalking the streets somewhere or other,' Muriel had replied, perhaps a little uncharitably. 'And at this time of year, any wind that blows is generally of an unpleasant nature.'

Flossie had sniffed and got on with making her pastry.

When she returned to the sitting room, Henrietta had kicked off her shoes and was reclining on the sofa, wiggling her toes by the fire. She appeared to have removed her stockings, revealing two plump legs like shins of beef.

'You took your time,' she said. 'By the way, I meant to tell you, I bumped into Sebastian last week.'

'Sebastian?'

'Yes, you must remember last Christmas. The youngest son of that judge.'

'Of course, he seemed like such a sweet boy.'

'I was just signing a few copies of my latest book at Hatchard's that day...'

'Really? They sell your books in Hatchard's?'

'Don't distract me with your little digs, madam. Oh, I brought you a copy by the way to add to your collection. It's in that paper bag.'

She kicked a rather battered specimen of a bag. Muriel pulled out a copy of *Champagne, Caviar and Murder!* by Henrietta Thayne.

'Sounds rather classy for you.'

'Yes, my publisher thought so too. He thought this may win over the critics at long last.'

Henrietta had had a lengthy writing career, churning out two or three books each year which, if they troubled the critics at all, were quickly dismissed as 'lurid potboilers'. She feigned nonchalance in the face of such slights especially when she witnessed the praise bestowed upon the woman she saw as her greatest rival, that no-good upstart Agatha Christie. They had once met at a drinks party where Henrietta cut her dead in an instant, until Agatha tapped her on the shoulder and hissed, 'Henrietta, dear, I do believe you've spilt crème de menthe down your front. I hope it doesn't stain.'

'Your news?' said Muriel, attempting to divert them both from plummeting headlong into Henrietta's literary tribulations.

'So I was signing copies of *Champagne, Caviar and Murder!* when Sebastian walked by. I waved and beckoned him in and, the long and short of it is, that I invited him round for supper.'

'Tonight?'

'Yes.'

'On Christmas Day?'

'Muriel, dear, don't be so vacant. I happened to think that, what with his own father being bludgeoned across the head on Christmas Day last year, they may not be having a good old family Christmas this year. He seemed at a loose end and, as you said, he is such a sweet boy.'

'And when should I expect him?'

Henrietta squinted at her watch, 'Oh, round about now, I should think.'

The doorbell rang on cue.

'Well, thank you very much for the notice.' Muriel looked round the room in panic, having barely cleaned up after dinner, as the doorbell rang again. She snatched her paper hat from the floor and as she left the room, snapped, 'If I were you, I'd put my stockings back on.'

Instead Henrietta poured the gin.

Out in the hallway she heard Muriel say, 'Sebastian, how lovely to see you. I'm afraid Henrietta only just mentioned you were coming, so you'll have to take us as you find us... Oh, thank you, whisky, lovely. Henrietta will be pleased... Do come through.'

Sebastian entered the room: a tall, pretty young boy with floppily artistic hair and pale blue eyes.

'I hope I'm not intruding. Miss Thayne invited me...'

'Oh, call me Henrietta, darling.'

'It's no trouble at all, if Henrietta could just make a little more room on the settee, there may even be somewhere for you to sit down.'

Like a beached something-or-other, Henrietta struggled to right herself. She swung her legs down, making as she did so, a noise not unlike flatulence.

'Oops, pardon me!' she giggled. 'Did I hear mention of whisky?'

Muriel got the drinks and wondered what on earth she was going to do for supper. They had had only a crown of turkey for dinner and there were slim pickings to be had. Perhaps if she poured enough drinks, no-one would notice the absence of food.

'So how are you?' asked Henrietta.

'Fine, I suppose. Oliver has had to go to his family in the country, we didn't think it proper for me to go as well. His father is a vicar, you know, he may not take too kindly to mine and Oliver's...'

'Friendship?' Muriel suggested.

He smiled ruefully. 'Yes, something like that. So I have been at a loose end in London. My brother Gerald is now firmly ensconced at Flettering Hall — utterly Lord of the Manor these days — and mother has shut herself away in the Dower House. Gerald inherited the lot in the end, apart from a few allowances here and there. He said I could visit any time, but rather in the way that he hoped I never did.'

'And what about your sister Hilary and — what was her name — Camille?'

'I believe Gerald received a postcard from her. Julia, my other sister, was visiting him at the time. I doubt her marriage is long for this world. She told me they were staying in Antibes, I think. Gerald tore the card to shreds. Now he's engaged to some frump from the local Conservative Party. Much more up his street than Camille.'

'It was a rather odd Christmas, wasn't it?' said Henrietta.

'That's something of an understatement.'

'Yes, but the thing I never understood,' said Sebastian, 'is how the two of you came to be there in the first place.'

Naturally, it had all been Henrietta's doing. On a howling November evening last year, she had been discovered assaulting Muriel's knocker at some ungodly hour and brandishing a letter.

'We've been summoned by a judge!'

Muriel, rather stunned to have another peaceful evening shattered by her old friend, popped on her glasses, grabbed the damp letter and said, 'Whatever do you mean?'

'Oh, don't worry,' said Henrietta, blithely helping herself to the decanter, 'I doubt he's cottoned on to anything from your past. Cheers!'

Muriel shook her head, choosing to ignore yet another of Henrietta's thinly-veiled jibes. 'Who on earth is Judge Flettering? And why does he want our help?'

'You must know him by reputation. He's often in the papers, known as the Hanging Judge. If there's anyone up before him who he can send to the gallows, he's whipping out his black silk before you can say, 'Orff with his head!''

'Why on earth would we help him?'

'I'm rather intrigued,' said Henrietta, pouring them both a drink this time. 'I met him once on the Riviera...'

'Torquay?'

'Monte Carlo, actually,' she said wistfully. 'I recall that he got a trifle 'heavy-handed' with me after one too many aperitifs. Not that he got anywhere, of course! Awful man! Hands as cold and probing as fish-hooks, if my memory serves me correctly; he got them stuck, in my opinion, into places no man should ever venture. Anyway, he has received one of those anonymous letters that are *toute la rage* with unfulfilled spinsters of a certain age.' She gave Muriel a knowing look. 'It claims he is to be murdered at his own Christmas party this year. Apparently, he heard tell of how we discreetly mopped up that mess at the Gaiety Theatre last spring and wondered if we could help him, rather than have the whole of Scotland Yard clod-hopping their way through his private life.'

Muriel sipped her sherry and said, 'I really don't think it's our cup of tea...'

On the morning of Christmas Eve Muriel and Henrietta found themselves packed on to a small train heading out from Paddington to the back of beyond. Snow was falling over London and, as they headed into the countryside, it grew heavier, the view becoming obscured.

'If I were him,' said Muriel, 'I'd simply cancel the whole damn thing.'

'Sorry? Miles away, have you got a light?'

'I meant if I received an anonymous letter, claiming to be from one of my family, I would hardly carry on blindly and invite them all to a big Christmas party, simply because it's tradition.'

'But it's not just that, is it? The Judge wants to know which of the scheming blighters has got the audacity to try and kill him.'

'And what if one of them succeeds?'

'That's hardly going to happen, is it? Not on our watch.'

The car that met them at the station struggled through the snow: the chauffeur subservient and apologetic about the weather. Then, through the blizzard, they could make out Flettering Hall. A huge brick monstrosity, it towered over the countryside and failed to look welcoming despite the weather.

'Looks like a loony bin,' said Henrietta, steeling herself with another cigarillo.

'Let's hope we don't get locked up.'

They trudged through the snow to the grand entrance where a flank of servants shivered under the portico and the Judge stood, already in evening wear.

'At last,' he said, a little disgruntled. 'Thought you weren't coming.'

Muriel eyed his big fleshy face with distaste; he was so pink that there was something obscene about him. She began to explain about the obvious hindrance of the weather, but the Judge simply said over her, 'Parrot will show you to your rooms, then there are drinks in the sitting room in half an hour. Then,' he said darkly, 'you can meet my family. Don't be late.'

Then he was gone.

Muriel and Henrietta followed the silent Parrot up the marble staircase, past an ostentatiously decorated Christmas tree.

'Whatever happens,' Muriel hissed to Henrietta, 'you do realise we are going to be holed up in here with a potential murderer.'

'Oh tish!' she replied. 'I have heard he has an unrivalled stock of whisky.'

Her eyes glittered like cheap baubles.

'Ooh, ta very much!' said Henrietta, helping herself to a proffered cocktail as they entered the sitting room. As she sailed into the room, Muriel was forced to rescue her escaping fox-fur.

'Ah, my final guests. Miss Henrietta Thayne and...'

'Miss Muriel Grey.'

'Of course.'

The sitting room was a veritable Christmas grotto: a smaller tree was surrounded by gaily wrapped presents, holly and ivy garlands festooned the walls and a choir trilled carols from a gramophone. But the atmosphere was anything but festive, and Muriel positioned herself near the fire to escape the chill.

There were four children. Gerald was the eldest and something nondescript in the City. He had aspirations of Parliament, the Conservatives of course, but all his ambition, as far as Muriel could see, was based on his father's connections. His fiancée was Camille who looked rather unsuitable for a Tory wife, with her bobbed raven hair and low cut scarlet dress. 'Used to be on the stage, you know,' said Henrietta, with a needless nudge, sending half of Muriel's cocktail over the hearth-rug. Next came Julia, who seemed of little consequence, married to a weasley little man named Harry, who had a rather odd gait, Muriel noticed, when he went to replenish his drink, which was often. She winced slightly as Henrietta barrelled up to them, barged into their conversation and stood so close that they clearly felt intimidated. With a thoroughly unappealing laugh Henrietta said, 'Oh, please excuse me a moment, I think Muriel wants a word.'

'Do I?'

'I've got the measure of them. Not a penny to their name. He claims he can't hold down a job due to his war wound from Flanders. War wound! Where I come from, that limp is just mincing. He could be our man. I suspect Harry is hiding some very insalubrious debts.'

'Keep your voice down.'

'Hello, I'm Hilary,' said a woman several years younger than Julia. 'The one that hasn't got away... yet.'

'Pleased to meet you.'

'I believe we have already met at my father's office on one occasion,' she went on, causing Muriel to splutter an apology. 'Don't worry, I'm just the little secretary, no-one ever notices me.' She turned her gaze upon her family. 'You met Harry then. Utter con artist if you ask me. Haven't the faintest idea what Julia sees in him. Anyway, welcome to Flettering Hall. I hope you enjoy the charade.' She picked up a gardening trug and a box of sugar cubes from a sideboard that was laden with vegetables. 'Off to see to the horses before dinner.'

Muriel gave a forced smile. 'Rather a blunt young thing, isn't she?'

'Isn't that just what you need when a murder is being plotted?' said Henrietta. 'That's the younger daughter. I believe the Judge uses her as some unpaid skivvy.'

'She looks a very homely type.'

'Fat, you mean. Dumpy.'

'Not exactly. More that she would probably come in handy during lambing season, that sort of thing.'

'I know exactly what you mean,' said Henrietta, though she didn't. 'That's the last one, over there. Sebastian, chatting to his friend from Oxford, Oliver.'

They watched them drawing on their cigarettes, then laughing at some private joke, casting furtive glances round the room.

'I think we've got the measure of them,' said Henrietta with one of her practiced looks as the dinner gong sounded. 'Where's the Judge's wife? Lady Anne?'

'I think that's her over there.' Muriel pointed at a bath chair, turned away to face the French doors. A withered hand hung over the side next to a discarded glass of sherry. Parrot entered and swiftly wheeled the bath chair round and scooted towards the dining room, Lady Anne passed the two of them with a dazed look on her face.

'She looks like she's made of desiccated coconut,' said Henrietta, as the Judge jostled them from the room.

The dining room was festively resplendent. A huge glazed ham — looking not unlike the Judge — dominated the ornately decorated table. Yet the atmosphere was still more funeral wake than Christmas party. Muriel and Henrietta found themselves marooned in the middle of the table, casually eavesdropping on what little small talk went on around them.

'Perhaps it's poisoned,' Henrietta whispered. 'They always say that's a woman's method of doing away with someone.'

'Hush! And don't drink so much claret. We may need a clear head.'

After the main course, the Judge stood up, more red-faced than ever as the fire roared behind him.

'I think I should say a few words,' he said, in that deep voice that had announced the death of many a desperate criminal. Lady Anne, who had picked up an ear-trumpet for a moment, quickly laid it aside again. 'I should say what a pleasure it is to have my family around me again at this time of year. I *should* say that, but I won't. I have here,' he said, brandishing a piece of paper, 'an anonymous letter, sent to me recently informing me that I am to be murdered this Christmas. The implication being that the person responsible is sitting round this very table.' The family all looked shiftily down at their napkins. 'Who to choose? Could it be you, Gerald? A man I have given every introduction to; got you memberships of all the right clubs and yet you have still never amounted to anything, sitting happily on my coat-tails, waiting for that inheritance to come your way. Why did I ever waste my time? And what a wife to have chosen. The lovely Camille, who spent her youth dressed in a few feathers and little else on stage, entertaining the denizens of the East End in some tawdry music hall. I can see what attracted you all right, but really?'

'Father, I...' spluttered a reddening Gerald, but the Judge simply waved his hand dismissively to silence him.

'Then there's Julia. Unassuming little Julia. I suppose you're just here because that dastardly husband of yours, the supposed war hero, has frittered away another of my 'investments' on some hare-brained scheme. Look at you, even in candlelight I can see that dress is nothing but rags and darning.'

They didn't even bother to speak.

'And Hilary. Dependable, dull, old Hilary. The only one not to fly the nest because no-one will have her. A waste of a life at my beck and call, a seething ball of resentment perhaps?' To give the Judge his due, she certainly looked that way. 'Then last of all, my youngest son, foppish Sebastian with his dreams of being an artist in London with his 'pal'. Should I remind you that I am a Judge and can make life for so-called people like you rather difficult?'

He looked round the table, almost triumphantly, then raised his glass. 'To my family!' he said, drained his claret, and stormed from the room. 'I shall be in my study.'

No-one really felt like pudding, except for Henrietta.

As the remnants of Christmas spirit fizzled damply away, Gerald and Harry went to play a bad-tempered game of billiards, leaving Julia to her needlework in the sitting room where Camille also sat, painting her nails. Sebastian and Oliver had retreated with brandies to the orangery, leaving just Hilary.

'Is he always like that?' said Henrietta, happily accepting a whisky.

'One does rather get used to the blustering old fool. The rather annoying part of it all is that he is right. Utter disappointments, the lot of us.' She laughed unhappily and lit a cigarette. 'I have to say though, it would rather serve the old devil right if one of us chose to bash his head in. He wouldn't be missed. Excuse me, I think the dog might need letting out.'

She disappeared from the room, nonchalantly blowing smoke rings.

'What on earth should we do?' said Henrietta. 'He's certainly got everyone in the mood to bump him off.'

'I don't know.'

'I could casually eavesdrop on everyone, find out what they're up to. I'm terribly good at that.'

'Yes, you are good at eavesdropping, I'll grant you, but you are hardly discreet. Besides, I think we all know what they will be talking about. They are hardly likely to be plotting murder over the billiard table.'

'So you think it's one of them?'

'I don't think anything at all,' Muriel sighed. 'Listen — from my bedroom, if we keep the door ajar —we may just be able to spy on the Judge's study. See who approaches him.'

'Oh, good idea. I'll bring supplies,' said Henrietta, grabbing the whisky decanter. Muriel looked at her disdainfully. 'Well, he won't miss it, will he? Not if he's going to be murdered...'

The scream came early in the morning. Muriel sat up in bed and, hearing a second scream followed by a heavy thump, jumped up, dragged on her dressing gown and vigorously poked Henrietta, who appeared to have fallen asleep in an armchair, decanter in hand. By the time they blearily made their way onto the landing, the whole family, bar Lady Anne, were gathered round the Judge's study.

'Who could have done such a thing? It's too, too awful!' whined Julia, clasping her hand to her mouth.

Now fully awake, Henrietta shouldered her way through. Gerald stood over the body of his father, who lay slumped, pale and dead on a chaise longue. His dressing gown had been untied to reveal his naked corpulence and, to top it all off, a huge carrot had been shoved in his mouth.

'He's supposed to be a snowman,' she said.

'What?'

'The carrot.'

'I really don't think ladies should be present here,' Gerald blustered, 'Parrot, could you take everyone downstairs, give them a brandy and then call the police.'

'Begging your pardon sir, we took the liberty of calling the police when we found the maid, Daisy, unconscious.' No-one seemed to give a fig about poor Daisy who was being dragged from the room by her ankles. 'Unfortunately, all the phone lines are dead.'

'Then send a boy to the town to get them.'

'Perhaps sir may care to look out of the window. Even in such an emergency, I fear sending anyone out in this snow would be to send them to their deaths. It is seven miles to Flettering.'

Gerald simply stood there as if his mind had run out of things to consider. Henrietta took the opportunity to gently draw him out of the room. 'You go and join the others, Gerald. We'll take care of all this. That's why we're here after all.'

Once he had mutely gone, she snapped the key in the lock and turned to Muriel.

'So?'

'Shouldn't we cover him up with something. It's rather off-putting don't you think?'

'Enough to even put me of my brekkers.' She grabbed an overcoat from behind the door and covered up the worst of him.

'Now, I've got some gloves in my handbag: go and get them.' Henrietta looked nonplussed. 'For goodness sake, you're the detective writer. When the police do get here, I don't want them moaning that two batty old women have destroyed the evidence.'

'Speak for yourself,' sniffed Henrietta, but went to get the gloves. She rather struggled to get her podgy hands into them. Muriel winced: they were goatskin.

'This isn't just a simple murder,' said Muriel, looking down at the Judge's pale face and the incongruous carrot. 'This is someone who wanted to humiliate the Judge.'

'Even though he's dead.'

'But whenever one of his family think of their dear old father, this is the image they will picture. His reputation is ruined forever.'

'It hardly matters to him, though, does it? He's dead to the world.'

'Unless the person, or persons, stripped him whilst he was alive. Perhaps they made him beg, or do something else.'

'This is typical of you, Muriel. One glimpse of a corpse and your mind heads straight for the gutter. It's rather early in the day for chatting about sexual perversions. But does that mean it was a woman?'

'Possibly. Or it could just as easily have been a man, someone who wanted to emasculate the Judge.'

Henrietta sniffed. She found Muriel's attempts at amateur psychology a little jumped-up at times. There was never any psychology in her books. Just simple greed, lust and, occasionally, wanton irritation. That was what drove people to murder.

Muriel bent down on the hearth-rug and stared intently at the Judge's unsightly head. 'Well, that's what killed him. He's had one heck of a wallop to the back of the head. Probably with something blunt, perhaps wrapped in something. There's hardly any blood.'

Henrietta lit a cigarillo. 'Do you mean like that poker lying on the floor over there with a bit of old sacking round it?'

'That would fit the bill, yes.'

'You are a veritable Sherlock today, aren't you?' A stray bit of ash fell on the Judge's face. 'Ooops! I'll blow it off, no-one will know. Maybe there are some clues on the desk.'

Among the papers chaotically strewn on the desk was a copy of his will. Gerald inherited the house, it seemed, but there were generous allowances made for all his children.

'Perhaps he was going to change it,' said Henrietta. 'He hardly seemed that enamoured with his brood last night. But someone got in first. Hello, what's this?'

She retrieved a large black book from the floor under the desk. 'It's a scrapbook. Cuttings of all his old cases.'

She was about to leaf through it when Muriel stopped her. 'What page was it open on?'

'Someone called Madame Desfarges. Some French woman he sent to her death. Seems to have caused a bit of a hoo-ha in the press.'

'Oh yes. I recall. Rather pretty, wasn't she? That must have been ten years ago, at least.'

'1918 according to the newspaper. She claimed to have acted in self-defence against some drunken brute but he was having none of it. She went to the gallows just before Christmas. Ah, look, she left behind a child, just twelve years old.'

'Boy or a girl?'

'Doesn't say.'

Muriel sat down in the desk chair and looked in front of her. 'What's this?' she said, head bent down over the blotter.

'A blotter,' said Henrietta, helpfully.

'No, this,' she said, pointing to a small blob of something red. 'It looks a little like blood.'

'How remarkable, but then again, he *has* had the back of his head bashed in. I think we can excuse a few stray drops of blood here and there.'

'But it hasn't soaked into the blotter.'

'Cheap blotting paper. I said to the stationer's I use just the other day that I thought their products had gotten awfully shabby of late. They muttered something about these dire economic times. I said that's no excuse for poor workmanship.'

Muriel wasn't listening, she was leafing through a diary.

'Anything interesting?'

'Not really, just rather curious. On almost every page, he seems to have an appointment at two o'clock but whoever it is, is simply recorded as a single initial. Look, V, L, E, C, V again.'

'Oh yes?' Henrietta's interest was a little piqued. 'Up to no good was he?'

'Judging by this pile of receipts for a hotel in Clerkenwell, he was not.' Muriel sat back for a moment. 'There's something about this, though, that is just too helpful.'

Henrietta stubbed out her cigarillo and glared at Muriel. 'What on earth do you mean?'

'Oh, probably nothing. Now, I think it's time we joined the others for breakfast.'

'Good idea, I'm ravenous.'

'By the way, I'd retrieve that fag end of yours. Otherwise the police will think that *you* did it.'

***

The family were all in the dining room, glasses of restorative brandy accompanying their breakfast. Someone had evidently informed Lady Anne, since she was lolling in her bath chair wearing what looked like a black sack. Her ear trumpet lay discarded.

'I don't think I could eat a thing, I really don't,' said Julia, a cup of black coffee shaking in her hand. 'I don't know how you can.' She eyed her husband's plate of Full English with distaste. He carried on regardless.

'Let's be realistic, Julia. He was bound to drop dead soon enough,' said Hilary, 'and none of us can pretend we liked him. I think it's rather splendid that one of us had the gumption to do him in.'

'How could you?' Julia spluttered.

'Yes, Hilary, that was a little uncalled for,' said Gerald. 'Mother is present.'

'And as deaf as a post,' said an unrepentant Hilary.

Camille was sitting at the table, painting her nails. 'Must you do that at the table, darling?' said Gerald. 'It does have the most frightful smell.'

'Murder or no, I don't see why I should sacrifice my nails.'

'Does anything other than the state of your nails go

round in that pretty little head of yours?' Hilary asked, slopping a couple of kidneys on her plate.

'Actually, yes, Hilary. Such as if you took just an ounce of care about your appearance and personal hygiene, perhaps you wouldn't be stuck in this Godforsaken hole for the rest of your life. I mean, look at you! Who in their right mind would have you?'

'Oh, *touché*. Now we all know what an utter bitch you really are!'

Gerald rose to his feet and was about to bluster something when Hilary interrupted, 'Don't bother, Gerry. I am off to see to the horses.'

Muriel watched her leave the room and couldn't help noticing that behind the disgruntled expression, her eyes were smiling.

'Anyway,' said Camille, carefully picking up her coffee so as not to damage her nails. 'I heard a lot of coming and going last night.'

'Did you?' said Henrietta.

'I was a little thirsty and was going to get a glass of water when I saw someone scurrying down the corridor. They were wearing white pyjamas, whoever it was. White with a blue stripe. So, at least I know it wasn't you, Gerald. I suppose it could have been Hilary. Heaven knows what she wears in bed.' She paused for a girlish giggle. 'An old workman's overalls, I expect. Then, of course, as I was returning, a door opened and closed and I heard two whispering voices. Two male voices. Couldn't have been you, could it Sebastian?' She raised her eyebrow at a quailing Sebastian, who glanced furtively at his friend, Oliver. 'I think I shall go for a lie-down, this is intolerably early, even for Christmas Day. I shall open my presents later, darling.'

She blew a perfunctory kiss towards Gerald as she left the room.

'Thank God I'm not a member of this accursed family just yet.'

Muriel inclined her head towards Henrietta and whispered, 'I think we have seen enough.'

'Have we?' she said, looking dumbfounded as a spoonful of boiled egg slipped down the front of last night's blouse.

'I'm not sure that I remember everything happening quite like that,' said Henrietta as she gulped down the last of a mince pie.

'But your memory can be a little hazy,' said Muriel, pouring only a spot of whisky into her empty glass.

Henrietta bristled and took hold of the bottle, 'Of course, you had to go and spin things out, didn't you? I was all primed and ready for the drawing room scene, you jabbing your finger at the murderer and revealing all, so to speak. But all you did was disappear and do some knitting.'

'I had to mull things over – go easy with that whisky Henrietta, we do have a guest – and knitting always helps me to get my thoughts in order. Besides, I had a nice chat with Sebastian here and we got to the bottom of what he and Oliver were up to that evening.'

'I think I can guess,' said Henrietta drily.

'The thing about the whole debacle was that it seemed to me that the murderer, or murderers, wanted to be found out. The artfully placed scrapbook, the appointment diary exposing his philandering, that stray drop of blood on the blotter which was, of course, nail varnish. They wanted us to know why they had done what they did. Of course, it was unlikely that Camille could have wrestled the judge's corpse on to the chaise longue by herself and Hilary, from the moment we arrived, was terribly keen for us to ealize how much she loathed her father. She even said it would serve him right if he were bashed over the head and, lest we forget, was even wandering round that night with a basket of carrots that she claimed were for the horses, rather than ramming down her father's throat. She dressed everything up as plain old bluntness, of course, and when I saw the playful banter between her and Camille, I saw there was much more to their relationship than I initially thought.'

'I can't say that I ever thought that the two of them were lovers!' said Sebastian. 'I can barely believe it now.'

'Oh, Muriel would,' said Henrietta. 'She has a very coarse mind.'

'And the scrapbook?'

'It came to me when I was negotiating a particularly difficult piece of ribbing in my knitting. The woman who the Judge hanged was Camille's mother. What better motive for revenge? Coupled with Hilary's years of drudgery and resentment and heaven knows what else at the hands of the Judge, well, that tipped the two of them over the edge. Simple as that.' Muriel coughed. 'Of course, I could have got it all wrong. That *has* happened before...'

'Yes, I remember,' sighed Henrietta. 'Utterly mortifying...'

Muriel revealed most of these facts on the morning of Boxing Day, sketching over a few of the less salubrious details for appearance's sake. By now the thaw had set in. In the background there was the steady sound of insistent dripping.

'Is this true?' demanded Gerald, his face as white as his mother's.

'Afraid so, darling,' said Camille, rather chirpily given the circumstances.

Hilary stood by her side. Framed against the window, they did rather resemble Laurel and Hardy.

'So,' said Hilary, lighting a cigarette and, for a moment, letting her composure slip as her hands shook, 'time to call the police is it?'

'I believe the phone lines are still down,' said Muriel.

'In the meantime, we have a proposition for you,' said Henrietta. 'We could just sit here playing party games until the police arrive, watch you being carted off to the cells and read every gory detail in the press about the case. Or, we could all pretend this never happened.'

'What on earth do you mean?' asked Julia.

'I doubt any of you really want to see Hilary and Camille hanged, do you? Despite what they've done. My proposition is that you simply bundle you father into bed, call in the trusty old family doctor and explain how you found him at the bottom of the stairs unconscious after a fall. I doubt the doctor would kick up a fuss, especially if you drop a few hints about the Judge's gratitude for his faithful services over the years – doctors are all money-grabbing pests after all. Get him to scribble a death certificate and the police will make the most rudimentary of investigations into the whole affair. We're talking gentry here, after all. Come New Year, you'll all be basking in your legacies and the whole thing could be forgotten.'

There was a stunned silence, broken only by the dripping from the guttering.

'But… but, that's scandalous!' Gerald spluttered. 'What would mother say?'

Lady Anne was asleep in her bath chair, gently snoring.

'Well, it's up to you. Scandal and shame forever more, or a few white lies and the whole thing blows over.' Henrietta lit a cigarillo breezily.

The family looked at each other, nervously exchanging glances, no-one seemed to wish to be the first one to speak.

'Now, if you'll excuse us, Parrot informs me that the roads may now just about be passable. Muriel and I really ought to be going.'

'But what about the police?'

'I'm afraid this is really all down to you now, we have done all that we can,' said Muriel, gathering up her handbag and knitting. 'Besides, it would look rather odd, wouldn't it? Two old busy-bodies turning up here out of the blue. Heaven knows, they would probably try and pin the whole thing on us!'

Henrietta snorted a laugh, nudged Muriel in the side and they turned to go. Parrot opened the door. As they left, Hilary mouthed a silent, 'thank you,' and Gerald could be heard to mutter, 'Of course, this means we'll have to tip the servants a few quid…'

***

'It all went to plan, I take it?' asked Muriel. 'We read the obituary in *The Times* and there was certainly no mention of foul play.'

'Oh yes, old Doctor Protheroe had been tending to our family since time immemorial. He can barely see a thing these days. Bless him, he was rather upset by the whole matter. He cheered up somewhat when Gerald sent him a cheque from the estate. I believe he's retired to Bournemouth now.'

Sebastian stared into the fire for a moment, as if the memory of aiding and abetting his own father's murderers had suddenly become too much for him.

'It was a shame you had to rush off like that,' he said at last. 'We rather needed some level-headed people to get us through the whole nightmare. Julia was a wreck, but we passed that off as grief.'

'The police would have been there soon enough and really, we didn't want to get mixed up in all of that,' said Henrietta. She gave Muriel one of those looks.

'I do see that, of course.'

No,' said Henrietta, giving his hand a patronising little pat, 'I really don't think that you do...'

Whisky, Henrietta?' said Muriel, giving her a friend a quick slap.

Sebastian looked a little mystified, wondering for a moment if something were being hidden from him, so Muriel cut in. 'Now, should I open the champagne I was saving for New Year, or is everyone tipsy enough for charades already?'

'I never play charades,' said Henrietta, 'and certainly not in a tweed twinset. I think Sebastian can cope with the truth this time.'

Muriel thought about looking daggers at her friend but relented. 'Go on then,' she said with resignation.

'True enough, Hilary did send the threatening letter, but it was just mischievous spite, and he did contact us as we said. However, when we visited his office, both of us resolved to have nothing more to do with him. He was a frightful human being after all.' Muriel and Sebastian nodded in agreement. 'After the interview, we met Hilary who was working in his office, and she gave us a few home truths about how despicable his behaviour was.'

'His sexual desires were not simply limited to women of easy virtue in a Clerkenwell hotel,' Muriel added.

Henrietta bristled. 'This is my turn, Muriel, you got the grand scene at Flettering Hall, after all! We saw how desperate she was to be free of her father and we simply offered to help.'

'To help? So it was you...?'

'Yes,' said Henrietta, lighting a cigarillo. 'We bashed him over the head and set the whole thing up to look like Camille and Hilary were guilty.'

'I'm sorry, but why would they take the blame? I don't quite understand.'

'Because we assured them we would get them off, simple as that.'

'But the rest of the family will think of them as murderers for the rest of their lives!'

'Look, Sebastian, they're kicking up their heels in Antibes and spending the inheritance on champagne. Do you really think they give a fig what the family think?'

Sebastian looked a little pale.

'She was worried about you, you know,' said Muriel, 'what with you both being of a... similar disposition. But now you know the truth. Perhaps you could pay her a visit in the New Year, you and Oliver.'

'But, that's all so...' he seemed lost for words, then his face broke into a smile, '...so marvellous! No wonder you wanted to leave before the police came!'

He raised his glass to them.

'We like to help where we can,' said Muriel with a comforting smile.

'Oh, stop acting like Mother Superior,' Henrietta snapped, 'and go and get that champagne!'

Gray Matters

Scott Handcock

People think they know me, all the time. I have the kind of face they've seen before (and truth be told, they probably have. I've been around).

I was born in the year of our Lord eighteen hundred and sixty-six. I've lived on this earth for almost one hundred and fifty years – always tall, strong, handsome, bright – but time, it takes its toll. My soul withers and decays while my body remains intact. And the world around you changes.

I've outlived so many people now; survived so many friends, so many family... My life's been like a boulder gathering moss: momentum builds and builds and builds until, eventually, you just can't stop yourself. No matter how much you want to. And the more I see of the world, the less I think I can go on the way I have. There's nothing left to see, nothing new or exciting to do. My life ended before it started... and I never knew.

My name is Dorian Christopher Gray. People think they know what that name means.

Perhaps they do.

Most people know the story: the man who sold his soul for eternal youth. But then, most people also assume that I was named after Oscar's book. In fact, it was the other way round.

It amused him so much, back then, dear Oscar: to place me in a world of degradation and corruption; to portray me as an advocate for hedonism. I used to be so innocent and naïve when I was younger. And yet life has an unfortunate habit of imitating art... however much forewarning we may be given. A downward spiral was inevitable for me, all told.

And yet, I never took my own life as the book suggests. Instead, I simply dared to go on living: the one thing Oscar couldn't bear to put me through. I thought I knew it all, back then. I truly believed that I could overcome the woes that dogged my namesake.

I outlived Oscar, Harry, and the rest of our social circle... but I went on to make new friends. I fought in the First World War, returned to London, raised a family. But they all died soon after... whereas I just kept on going: the only constant in an ever-changing world. And the only thing I recognize to this day.

I remained just as I always had been: a young and beautiful man, but a man with unique properties. I attracted the attention of governments and mercenaries. I was used as a secret weapon, for a time, which seemed rather exciting. It was something fresh and new and different: truly, a life to be envied! So I thought.

But the rest of the world moved on while I stayed still. Then, as the years marched on, attitudes changed. All the taboos that I'd indulged in when I was younger slowly became more and more acceptable and accepted, and the thrill of undertaking them diminished. Sex, drugs, violence, men, women... suddenly nothing was shocking, and nothing could shock. And I ended up feeling normal for the first time in decades. Even when I was practicing the extreme, there was someone else beside me doing the same. But for them it was still a novelty.

Normality's a dreadful word, and an even worse sensation. It's like everyone else is suddenly catching up. They're doing things I've done for years, things that can't excite me any more, no matter how hard I try. I'm lost and alone, in a world that doesn't care... about anything. Least of all me.

Occasionally, there's hope though. Sometimes you'll take refuge in a bar on a cold winter night – anything to shelter from the rain, you tell yourself. And who knows, for once, you might meet someone who doesn't care for you in the slightest. They're not remotely interested in your good looks, or your good clothes; they're not bewitched by your appearance or your status. And suddenly, you're caught off guard. You're able to engage in regular conversation without any of the pressures of attraction or mild flirtation.

However, to my regret, such encounters are strangely fleeting. If you attempt to show an interest in another, they simply assume you want something more. Either you want to chat them up, or take them home – ideally both. And sometimes that's what they're looking for – only not with you. Making that night a waste of both your time and theirs.

And so, on such occasions, people usually say their goodbyes after half an hour of 'conversation'. They thank you for the drinks you've kindly bought them, but they've suddenly and spontaneously just remembered that they've somewhere else to be.

Nothing is ever simple any more. But then, perhaps it never has been, never will be...?

There are the others, of course: the people who *are* interested, and make a move on you the moment you're through the door. Usually these people don't look quite as good as you, or their grasp of the English language barely registers. Neither of which is necessarily a problem, but neither are they unique. And when you're looking for something fresh and new and challenging – something rare and somehow stimulating – those things tend to matter.

Of course, such people are rarely looking for anything enduring or remotely worthwhile. All they desire is an evening of cheeky flirtation across a bar, occasionally glancing back to a mob of drunken onlookers and acquaintances, none of whom actually care who they might be with. Sometimes these exchanges might end with an ill-judged kiss as you depart. Maybe even an attempt to share a cab until, for various reasons, you both decide it's more convenient to hop out together at theirs. (You'll either walk the rest of the way, or just pop in to chat over a coffee. Not that anyone ever does. It's all part of the game.)

Once, it was exciting because it was all so unpredictable. Now, it's merely the social equivalent of painting-by-numbers. The moment you leave that bar, I think you both know where you'll end up. Which is normally in the arms of another human being, in a sweaty dissatisfied heap on someone's sofa.

An hour later, and you're calling another cab. You wake up the next day, as if nothing ever happened... in your own bed and in your own home.

Alone.

There is something peculiarly safe about the games that people play: perhaps it's in the knowledge that you can escape at any moment, that you have the power to leave whenever you choose. But there's no danger in that – knowing you're in control. So occasionally, you venture beyond your comfort zone, try something new. Or something you've forgotten you ever did.

People rarely come into my home, as you might imagine. I tend to lead a very private life. If people get too close, then there's the risk that they might ask too many questions. And yet, it's that closeness I now crave more than anything else. It's the risks I miss; the risks that make life exciting and unpredictable.

Perhaps people are fooled by my youthful looks? Perhaps people don't think I'm able – or even wanting – to offer anything more? They imagine all I want is something instant, crude and carnal. They can see it in my eyes: the life I've led; those pleasures I've indulged in.

I am, at heart, a base and soulless creature. Maybe I don't deserve that sort of life.

But it is not my place to judge my situation. I would rather have others judge me, as they do. So from time to time, I dare to lay myself on the line. I risk my secrets getting out and being discovered. And for the first time in years, I feel strangely, remarkably alive. Terrified, yes, but *alive*.

I go to the bar of the moment and sit alone, watching the doors as people enter: men, women, couples, groups... Then one of them catches my eye: a man. A young man...

He's tall, slim... attractive in an unconventional sense; a little quirky. For the next fifteen minutes, I find myself glancing back at him and –to my surprise – he's glancing back. We keep on meeting the other's gaze across the room, until eventually he dares to make a move.

He crosses over and places an order with the barman. Just a single pint. He's drinking alone, it seems. Then he turns to me, and holds out a hand to introduce himself.

His name's Dominic, he tells me: a postgraduate student, studying a Masters degree in American History and Literature. He's much the same age as I seem: twenty-four, perhaps twenty-five. Dark hair, blue eyes... smart and chatty, too. He finds my name amusing – the book, it's one of his favourites – though he thinks I had the cruelest parents in the world.

He isn't wrong.

We talk about nothing but nonsense for a good half hour or so, neither one of us seemingly sure where this is heading. He's meant to be meeting friends in town, he tells me, before disappearing onto the street for a quick cigarette. When he returns, he tells me that he's texted them to say that he's running late. But we both know he won't put them off forever.

Eventually, he makes his move to leave, and we end up swapping numbers (his suggestion). He calls mine to check it's genuine, which is... reassuring. Then he leaves the bar, out the door, and back into the bitter chill of that winter night, rolling up another cigarette as he goes.

I remain in the bar for the next few hours, of course, looking back on this encounter. Occasionally others try to start fresh conversations: a flurry of women, mostly – I buy them a drink, or they buy me one – but it's late and they're already worse for wear. Aggressive flirtation ensues, followed by frantic apologies, and by midnight, I'm back on the streets, wandering home beneath a drizzle of icy rain.

Nothing gained, but nothing lost, I tell myself. Every cloud has a silver lining. Then, there's a faint vibration in my pocket. It's my phone: a text from Dominic. It asks if I'm still in town, he's heading home. Wondered if I'd like a final drink before he calls it a night?

I don't even know his surname yet.

I decide not to reply, not yet, and start walking briskly back the way I came. I give myself five minutes before replying – I don't want to seem too keen. Besides, I'm enjoying the thrill of something new and unexpected. I want this sensation to last as long as possible: the uncertainty of two young men in a busy city (well, one young man). Maybe I'll meet him, maybe I won't. I could still head home. I'm not sure I want to, but I could. That's all that matters. Then another text: he's up by Covent Garden. I reply: I'm round the corner. But it's another ten or fifteen minutes before I find him.

He's standing alone, outside a coffee shop, checking his phone. Keeping his head down, looking busy. I walk up to him and say hello, and instantly the phone's thrust back inside his pocket. He greets me with a smile and a hug, which I reciprocate.

We ask about each other's respective evenings as we wander, searching the heart of the city for somewhere to drink. I can't comment for him, but I certainly lie through my teeth about what I've been up to. I suspect he knows it too. But still, he smiles and nods, showing an interest.

We carry on like this for another twenty minutes, politely laughing and smiling as appropriate, disregarding everywhere we pass as being either too crowded or too noisy for the time of night. There was a time I'd have considered this boring and unadventurous, but now... now I'm strangely fascinated... precisely because it's not what I would have ever done before.

His friends got pissed, he tells me, rolling another cigarette along with his eyes. He knows how they'll end up. I tell him I know exactly what he means. (Not that I do, it's been an age since I called it a night – but he appreciates the sentiment.)

We're now somewhere near Leicester Square, and nowhere appeals. Perhaps it's a sign, he says. Maybe it's time to go our separate ways. Unless...?

He trails off, but that's my cue to make a suggestion... which is when I surprise myself – and him – by inviting him home, to my place.

I go through all the protocol, of course, as he's expecting. At first, I suggest sharing a cab, but I'm heading to Kensington, he's heading to Lewisham. So why doesn't he come back to mine? I have spirits in the cupboard, wine in the fridge, beer if he'd prefer it. Or we could just sit and drink coffee and tea, and talk until the sun comes up.

Talking's good, he tells me, as we hop into a cab. But then we fall strangely silent. Talking isn't that good, it seems, when you're sitting behind a stranger. Have you had a good night, he asks. So we both say yes and leave it at that.

That silence lasts until we reach our destination, when I have to ask the drive about the fare. Dominic offers to pay, of course, but I take care of it. And I suspect, from the look on his face, he's rather relieved.

I pay and tip the driver a fair amount, then step out onto the street, where I find Dominic just staring up and down. He doesn't know where I'm taking him, of course. To him, it's just a street of terraced buildings. Line after line of grand Edwardian homes, most of them converted into apartments.

But not mine...

I lead him up the steps to my front door, and I realise it's been years since I last invited anyone into my home. But then, that's not without good reason.

My heart's already beating slightly harder, apprehensive at what he'll make of my home... and me.

I show him in and quickly close the door behind us, leading him through to the living room. He comments on the décor as we walk, and something in his voice suggests he doesn't believe it's entirely to my taste. And yet it was, once, every last bit of it: all the furniture and trinkets; Peruvian armchairs and Chinese puzzle balls; first editions of all the greats and not-so-greats. Even a coat stand I once stole from the Moulin Rouge, back in the day (which, admittedly, I'm not all that fond of). Something from every corner of the globe, for every year I've lived. My tastes may change, but they serve to remind me who I was and who I can be... and who I might be once again.

I don't tell him any of that, of course, it would only alarm him. Instead, I offer to take his coat, which he promptly removes, exposing a snugly-fitted tee-shirt underneath (I pretend not to notice). I busy myself by opening a bottle of red – a rather lush and spicy Shiraz with quite a kick to it – then I tease him with a small amount to taste. He detects the warmth of the spices instantly, as you'd expect, but the other flavours are lost on him (a shame)...

Inevitably, we drink, and we try to make conversation – but our words are routinely punctuated by the creak of the leather sofa beneath our bodies. I try to shift my weight, to make myself more comfortable and more stable, but the creaking persists throughout. Dominic politely suggests I might like to stop talking if it's proving a problem. Then, when I continue our conversation, he makes sure that I stop talking – less politely.

His lips taste faintly of tobacco and wine as they meet with mine, and his left hand rises to tilt my face closer into his. I briefly pull away to set down my glass of wine, then run a hand through his long dark hair, a hand that then comes to settle – somewhat awkwardly – on his shoulder.

He laughs as he withdraws from me, apologizing. He never normally does this sort of thing, he says, embarrassed. I tell him I don't believe that for a moment – but he insists, and for a split-second I almost believe him.

Of course, Dominic makes the most of the opportunity. He catches me off-guard, and pins me down, planting his lips on mine and pulling me into him.

Waves of heat beat off him, radiating the narrow space between us. I must feel so cold to him, but if I do, he doesn't care or doesn't notice. Instead, he positions his body over me again, and the ancient sofa groans and squeaks in protest. I laugh as he makes to kiss me, and I suggest he might prefer somewhere... quieter.

He agrees.

I lead him to my room at the top of the house, and within moments his hands are running through and tugging at my hair, and my lips are clamped to his. I lift his tight red tee-shirt over his head, slipping my hands around his waist and down his back, as he struggles with the buttons on my shirt. He curses quietly till I help him, then our clothes are cast aside. He pushes me back onto my bed, running his tongue along my body, down my chest, rising up to kiss me again and again...

I don't know how long this lasts. I can feel his teeth tracing patterns along my torso, down my stomach. His fingernails dig deep into my flesh, pulling me closer, thrusting his body into mine. He nuzzles his jaw against my neck, nipping along my throat. I know that he's leaving bruises, but then I also know that they won't be there come the morning. Not that it matters. The sensations are new, at least with him. And for once, they're under my roof. He has control.

We go on like this for hours, or so it seems. I think we both lose track of time. But there's no sense he wants to leave. Instead, I lie there, holding him for a while. I don't want to let him go. And suddenly, I'm in control without even realising. Again.

I can feel his hand as it settles across my chest, he holds me back. So we lie there, in each other's arms. Together...

Then morning comes, inevitably: the sun bursts through the window, waking me up... and somehow, I'm alone. Dominic's side of the bed is neatly folded. His clothes and boots have vanished from the floor.

It's as though he was never there.

I stumble through to the kitchen then back to the living room – where I find him, sitting quietly. He's obedient, polite; curious without being too intrusive. In the cold light of day, my portrait is clearly visible, suspended – as it is – above the hearth. And now he's staring at it, dumbstruck. Maybe even awed?

It's been a lifetime since I allowed anyone to look upon that painting. Even now, after so many years, it still revolts me. The withered old flesh and mottled skin; the broken veins and scars... a terrible secret written in every wrinkle, every crease: marks for every year I should be dead. That creature stares down at me impassively, day after day. He watches me from its frame, judging me for the life I've inflicted upon him.

After so long, he is truly a grotesque beauty. He is a parody of life: an old and bloated man, smug and satisfied beyond his years. The man I should have been.

I've been in the room a minute now, and the boy's not said a word. He's simply watching the painting awkwardly, almost as though it's looking back at him. I move to sit beside him, and he rewards me with a passing glance... but nothing more. Instead, he simply nods toward the portrait.

Could it be that Dominic actually understands me? He recognizes what and who I should really be, beyond my looks?

For a single, fleeting moment, there's a sensation of simultaneous hope and dread that I know I've not felt in many years: the fear of someone discovering my secret. But also maybe – potentially – accepting who I am...

He leans towards me for a moment, resting a hand across my knee, and eventually he dares to break that awkward silence. He acknowledges what he's been staring at all this time: the same thing that's been staring back at me.

Where did you get it? he asks. Then, what's it supposed to be? He doesn't recognize me after all, it seems. He thinks it's some form of abstract (not to his taste).

Perhaps that's for the best.

I fob him off completely; tell him it's the work of some lesser-known artist from a long, long time ago. He says it doesn't go with the rest of the room, and I'd agree with him. It doesn't. But it belongs there, more than I do. And for that reason, it remains.

The awkwardness continues, and I realize that the silence wasn't terror or surprise. It wasn't the sudden shock of understanding who I was. It was just the guilt of a one-night stand. I've played the game too long, I know the signs.

He isn't sure when he should leave, and so suddenly I'm in control again. He's making idle conversation, but neither of us really engage in any way. He's just doing his best to be polite which is somehow sweet. Painful and excruciating, but sweet.

He asks if I have a boyfriend. I say no... an honest answer, for once.

I ask him the same question. There's a tacit obligation. But he doesn't answer, and I understand at once. Not that I care.

It is a simple, swift exchange. We probably have a fair amount in common, truth be told, but neither of us try to explore that any more. We just want the game to end. So he makes his excuses, as you'd expect – he has to leave, a lot to do – but we promise each other we'll catch up some other time. Just for coffee. It would be good to get to know each other – as friends. Just friends.

I know we won't, but he makes me promise him all the same. Even as I close the door behind him, I've already received a text. I delete it without reading it, of course. It's better for him that way. Better for the mysterious 'Dominic' in the long run.

I walk through my empty home again, back to the living room, where I'm all alone, as ever... just me and that ancient, mildewed godforsaken portrait.

I stare up at its disgusting visage, just as it stares down on mine. The corners of its crooked mouth have twisted upwards since I last left the room: a mocking, vicious smile that I recognise all too well. That portrait knows what I secretly yearn for, just as it knows I'll never find it. And that amuses it... Him... Me.

He relishes the pain of other people, especially me. He knows how I truly think and what I feel – he experiences the same things I do, after all. Every last pang of my guilt, and shame; every last scar from every fight I've ever started. He's lived my life for me, without ever being able to guide it. And my pain amuses him no end for that very reason.

Don't misunderstand me. When my heart aches, his heart aches tenfold. He endures where I could not. And I am grateful to him for that. All my emotions are locked away, in him, so no one ever has to see them. Meaning I can wear my mask against the world: an image of the man I want to be, the man I want people to believe I truly am.

But mine is a life without consequences. And a life like that is dangerous.

People think they've seen it all, but believe me, they really haven't. They don't live long enough to see. Instead now, they see too much.

There's no longer anything unique or new, nothing that you could claim to be exceptional. And worse than that – far worse – nothing is now forbidden... There are no more risks to take.

And so here I am – Dorian Christopher Gray – the same man I always have been. The world's grown up and older, but I haven't. I'm still waiting to discover something new... or for someone else to discover me. Because when they do – *if* they do – who knows how they'll react? Indeed, who knows how I will...?

A new experience, teasing me, with everyone I meet – the prospect of being exposed somehow *exciting* me. Maybe one day soon, I'll find it, or they'll find me?

There's plenty of time...

The Reason

Rupert Smith

Greg pushed long, tanned fingers through his tousled black hair and squinted up into the light. Even with his Dolce and Gabbana aviator shades, the sun was dazzling – the brilliant sun of a perfect English summer's day, beating down over the garden of his Hampshire home. He had not heard anyone approach – somewhere nearby a blackbird was singing, the water in the pool was lapping, and there was the buzz of a distant lawnmower from the other side of the house. Footsteps made no sound on the rolling green lawns that surrounded Amblingframpton Hall, dissolving into woods that stretched as far as the eye could see. And yet, standing over him, a black silhouette framed by dazzling light, there was a man.

For a moment, Greg felt a frisson of fear tingling over his smooth, oiled skin. He was vulnerable, lying there on a lounger, nothing to defend himself with but a highball glass of rapidly-warming campari and soda, nothing to cover his gym-toned body but a tiny pair of black Speedos. If an intruder had made it past the security gates, had come to kidnap him... If he shouted for help, no one would hear him.

He shaded his grey-green eyes with one slender brown hand. 'What do you want?' he said, keeping his voice cool and even.

'Mr O'Donnell?'

'Yes.'

A hand moved towards him from the darkness of the body, the light catching the bracelet of a gold watch. 'Waverley Moncrieff.' The voice was as warm as the sun, as dark as the shadow he cast. 'From Moncrieff and Moncrieff.' Although Greg couldn't see the face, he sensed a smile. 'Your solicitors.'

Greg sat up. 'Of course! Mr Moncrieff. I'm so sorry. I had completely forgotten our appointment.'

'No one answered the door so I took the liberty of coming round. I kind of guessed you might be in the garden on a day like this. Or in the pool...'

Greg jumped to his feet; thank God he hadn't been sunbathing naked, as he so often did when the staff had their afternoon off. But wait – this wasn't Moncrieff, surely. The family lawyer who had overseen probate of Greg's uncle's will – who had supervised his unexpected inheritance of Amblingframpton Hall and the millions that went with it – was a fat old man of fifty at least, and this... Well, this was something very different. Long legs, slim hips, broad shoulders, a lightweight charcoal suit of Italian cut, a tailored white shirt, a long, golden neck rising from the collar to a square jaw lightly dusted with stubble... blond hair, parted at the side, combed over like a sheaf of golden wheat... and those eyes, piercing blue, ironic, twinkling...

'I'm his son,' said Moncrieff, as if he'd read Greg's mind. 'I've recently been taken on as a partner. I'll be handling your business from now on.' Was it Greg's imagination, or did those blue eyes flicker down to the front of his Speedos? 'I hope that's okay with you.'

'Sure, sure.' Greg felt his heart beating faster. 'Look, let me just run inside and change...'

'Don't bother on my account,' said Waverley Moncrieff, holding up a Louis Vuitton briefcase. 'I've got everything I need right here.'

'Okay. Come over to the pool. There's a table there.' He led the way across the lawn, conscious at every step of Waverley's gaze. They sat, and Waverley clicked the briefcase open.

'I won't beat about the bush, Mr O'Donnell. 'We're in serious trouble here.'

'What?' Greg felt icy fingers down his spine, as surely as if Waverley had touched him. 'What kind of trouble?'

'It's your aunt. She's filed a claim of undue influence.'

'You can't be serious.'

'She's saying that you and your Uncle Oscar... well.'

'That's bullshit!'

'She has pretty compelling evidence, Mr O'Donnell.'

'That's not possible.'

'Certain photographs...'

'They're fakes. They've got to be.'

'I'm afraid they're not.'

Greg sprang to his feet. 'Christ, Moncrieff, whose side are you on? I mean, I've paid a fortune to your father over the last twelve months. The least I deserve is some kind of respect. Some kind of trust.'

'Hey, hey.' Waverley reached across the table and laid a hand on Greg's arm; an electric thrill coursed through his veins. 'Of course I'm on your side. But I'm just saying we have a fight ahead of us.'

'You mean... I could lose the estate?'

'It's possible.' He had not moved his hand. Greg sat, and put his hands over his face. 'But we can fight it together, Mr O'Donnell.'

'For God's sake, call me Greg.' Their eyes met as a sudden, cool breeze sent ripples across the blue surface of the pool. Greg shivered. 'It's getting cold. Let's go indoors.'

***

It was dark in the living room after the brightness of the sun, and for a moment Greg could see nothing. He was acutely aware that he was alone, almost naked, with a fully-clothed stranger.

'Strip.'

The word came out of the gloom, harsh and commanding. Greg turned round and saw Waverley silhouetted in the doorway – the broad shoulders, the narrow waist, the square head slightly haloed where the light caught his blond hair. One hand clutched the front of his trousers.

'What did you...'

'I said strip.' Waverley stepped forward. 'Unless you want me to do it for you.'

Greg felt a sudden rush of blood as his cock began to stiffen, stretching the sheer black fabric of his Speedos. 'I don't think...'

Waverley stepped closer – two feet away now, close enough for Greg to see the flatness of his stomach, the bulge at his groin. The pale blue eyes were hooded, the full lips damp. 'Do it,' said Waverley, 'now.'

His head spinning, Greg could only obey. He hooked his thumbs inside the waist and jerked down, releasing his half-hard cock. It pulsed for a moment in the half-light, and then began to soar through the air, reaching full erection in less than ten seconds. Both men watched it climb.

'Not bad,' said Waverley, reaching out and taking it in his hand, squeezing it appreciatively. 'Not bad at all.' His hand moved up and down; Greg's knees buckled. 'But you want to see a real man's cock? Huh? Do you?'

He managed to stammer 'Yes', as Waverley pulled him closer, one hand in the small of his back, his lips finding Greg's neck, blond stubble scratching against sun-warmed skin. Greg fell into the embrace, his arms around Waverley's shoulders. 'Oh God,' he said. It had been a long time.

Waverley yanked the Speedos down to Greg's knees, hobbling him, and pushed him backwards. He lost his footing, and landed on the sofa, his cock bobbing in the air. Waverley stood before him, feet planted a yard apart, and began to unzip his charcoal grey trousers.

'This,' he said, one hand diving in behind white shirt-tails, 'is what a real man's cock looks like, rich boy.' What he pulled out was only half-hard, but already it was longer and thicker than Greg's, a pale cylinder of flesh with a blue vein running along the back, branching over the foreskin, from which a helmet of coral pink was emerging. Greg swallowed.

'Think you can take it?'

Greg looked up, his brown eyes gleaming under long, dark lashes. Waverley's strong hand gripped his curly hair and pulled him in. Greg opened his mouth and let the head of Waverley's cock rest on his tongue, feeling the warmth and weight of it, tasting the salty, masculine flavour. Their eyes met for a moment, Waverley's nothing more than a pale gleam of blue, and then Greg's lips closed around his cock and started moving down, taking it an inch at a time, until his nose was pressed against the cold metal of the zipper. He could go no further – but, inside his mouth, Waverley's cock was continuing its journey, growing longer, thicker, harder, moving deeper into Greg, opening his throat, stretching his lips, filling him... He wanted to move back, to breathe, but Waverley's hands were clamped to the back of his head, holding him down, caressing and possessing him. Greg's hands found Waverley's steel-hard thighs, as thick as young tree trunks, feeling the ridges and grooves of muscle as the man tensed, driving his dick deep inside him.

Finally the hands released him, Greg pulled back an inch or two and drew air through his nose, filling his lungs for the next descent, like a swimmer about to dive for pearls.

'That's a good boy,' said Waverley, his voice rough and low. 'Get it nice and hard. And then you know what I'm going to do.'

Greg could not speak, but the increased pace of his sucking was all the answer Waverley needed.

He pulled out suddenly, the vacuum sucking Greg's cheeks in, a strand of saliva still connecting tongue to cockhead. He grabbed Greg's ankles and yanked them in the air, then spat in his hand and smothered the saliva over his wet prick. That was all the lubrication he was going to get. Bracing himself with bent knees, he pulled Greg's arse into line, positioned himself between his hairy buttocks, now damp with sweat, found the target and pushed.

The pain was sharp and intense, but Greg bit his lip, breathed deeply and waited for it to subside. Waverley was inside him – all of him – and gradually the sharp agony of penetration faded, and a warmth began to flood Greg's body, a fire kindled deep in his guts as Waverley began, slowly, to fuck him.

***

Detective Inspector Michael Reynolds was having a bad morning. He was hungover for starters – but that was nothing new, he was hungover most days, had been ever since his wife kicked him out of the house and moved her new bloke in – a bloke he once thought was his friend. Now he found it hard to sleep in an empty box of a one-bedroom rented flat, traffic roaring along the A-road all night long, without dosing himself with alcohol. Scotch at first – but that smelt too much in the morning. Now he was on to vodka – just as effective, and almost odourless. A real drinker's drink.

He got a bollocking from the DCI when he got in – ten minutes late for a briefing, ten lousy fucking minutes, and despite his carefully cooked-up story about a road traffic violation he could tell that nobody on the team believed a word. No, they all thought, that's just Mike Reynolds screwing up again. Wife kicked him out, can't say I blame her, and now he's going to pieces. Unfit to lead an investigation. Leaning too much on his DCs, everyone covering up for him until there's no place left to hide.

'So what have we got, boss?' He tried to sound capable, controlled. The DCI cocked an unconvinced eyebrow, and returned to his papers.

'Reports of a domestic in one of the big houses out on the downs.'

Mike knew the kind of places, and the rich bastards who lived in them. People with staff, and holiday homes, and trophy wives. 'A domestic? What's that got to do with CID, boss?'

'Uniform's reporting suspicious circumstances.'

'Dead body?'

'Not as yet, Mike.' The DCI scowled at his papers again. 'Can't make a lot of sense from their report, to be honest with you. Need a couple of you to go out there and find out what's going on. Could be a waste of time.' He put his papers down and smiled. 'And since you've shown such an interest, Mike, perhaps you could handle this one for me.' Sniggering from round the table; good old Reynolds, getting stuck with some domestic that Plod can't handle. How long before he was booted out of CID? How long before he was just another bitter ex-copper with a shitty security job and a bottle-of-spirits-a-day habit?

'Sure. Sounds interesting.'

'Take Jefferson.'

Mike felt himself blushing.

'Off you go, then. What are you waiting for?'

Mike looked across the table to where Detective Constable Terry Jefferson, all five foot six of red-headed, freckle-faced, pug-nosed Irishman, sat on the edge of a table, legs swinging off the floor.

'C'mon then Jefferson,' he said, hoping his voice didn't waver. 'Let's go.'

Damn the boss – assigning Jefferson to him. The new boy, only up from uniform three months ago – and already he'd caused Mike Reynolds too many sleepless nights. Ever since that piss-up at the pub when they'd been celebrating the end of a big, messy drugs case, and Mike had a few too many and ended up locked in a toilet cubicle with Jefferson on his knees, doing what nobody had done to him for way, way too long...

'So, what have we got?' They were driving out of town, away from the drab grey blocks of flats, the broken marriages and disappointments, towards the lush rolling green of the countryside, where money smoothed away every problem.

'Not sure, sir.' Terry was sitting sideways in the passenger seat, one leg crooked up, his jacket unbuttoned. Mike found it hard not to glance down. 'Uniform made it sound weird. Noise of a struggle – shouting, banging, one neighbour thought she heard a shot. House is locked up at the front, but the back door was open. One of those big places, you know, french windows, a swimming pool...' He stretched. 'Sounds nice.'

'And inside?'

'That's the weird bit. One room's locked up, and when the call came they hadn't yet been able to break in.'

'What? Why the hell not?' Mike felt his head pounding; it was too hot in the car, and the job was a nonsense, and Terry Jefferson's smile and freckles were making it worse. He opened the window.

'They tried to break it down, sir, but there's some kind of security system in place.'

'And there's supposed to be someone inside?'

Terry shrugged, and leaned his head towards the window, rubbing his short red hair. 'We'll soon find out. In the meantime, it's nice to be out of the office, isn't it?'

'Guess so.'

Terry loosened his tie; Mike caught a glimpse of golden fuzz on his neck. 'Away from everyone else.'

Mike scowled; this was not what he needed. Not today, with his head pounding, a meeting with his solicitor to discuss the divorce the only thing he had to look forward to... 'So what does that tell you, Jefferson?'

'Sorry, what?'

'A locked room. Sounds of a struggle, possible gunshot.'

'Hostage situation?'

'Possibly.'

'Sounds cosy.' Terry grinned, showing slightly crooked teeth, one gold.

'And how would you suggest we handle it?'

'I can think of a few ways.'

Mike stared at the road ahead.

'We isolate the scene, we effect entry, and we try to save lives and minimise injury. Then, depending on what we find, we get forensics in.'

'Good.'

'Meanwhile, we try to enjoy ourselves.' He nudged Mike with his knee. 'Sir.'

There were four squad cars outside Amblingframpton Hall, parked in a fan shape on the gravel drive. There was still plenty of room for Mike – room for a whole fleet, if necessary. Whoever lived here had money to burn.

'Tell me what I need to know,' said Mike to the uniformed sergeant outside the front door. His head was clearing – adrenalin was kicking in, and now he was out of the car, away from Terry Jefferson and his damned smiling Irish eyes, the air seemed easier to breathe.

'Householder is a Mr Greg O'Donnell. Twenty nine years old, unmarried.' He made a show of referring to his notes. 'Known to be homosexual.'

'Go on.'

'Recently inherited this place from his uncle. There's been a certain amount of unpleasantness over the will.'

'And have they got the fucking door open yet?'

They were in the hall now. 'As you see, sir...' Three men in white protective suits were taping plastic sheeting over a frame, constructing a protective porch around the heavy wooden door beside the staircase. 'Steel shutters behind the wood. Same with the windows.'

'Why would a house like this need a panic room? What's he got in there?'

'Don't know, sir, but we'll find out soon enough. They're getting ready to blow it.'

'Anyone seen coming or going?'

'Not as far as we know. No cars parked in the vicinity. We found O'Donnell's diary in there.' He cocked his head towards a room at the end of the hall. 'Mentioned an appointment with his solicitor today.' He checked his notes. 'Moncrieff and Moncrieff. We rang them. Said he never turned up.'

'What time?'

'Two o'clock.'

'And what time did neighbours raise the alarm?'

'Shortly after twelve.'

'I see.' Mike scratched his chin; he hadn't shaved this morning, and it made a sound like sandpaper. 'I'd better take a look at this diary. Something doesn't add up.'

The first thing that hit them was the smell. Even before the rank smoke from the explosives had cleared it was there, beating out of the room like noise – a thick, rich smell of spoiled meat, and something higher, metallic, that Mike recognised as blood.

'Fuck,' he said, and gagged, getting a handkerchief to his mouth just in time. He swallowed his own vomit, and his mouth flooded with acrid saliva. He spat into the handkerchief, balled it up and put it back in his pocket. Behind him, Terry was doubled up, clutching his guts.

'When's the last reported sighting of Mr O'Donnell?' said Mike, cold sweat breaking out on his brow. He had to go in. Every cell in his body wanted to run, but he had to go.

'Cleaner saw him yesterday, sir,' said the uniformed constable.

'Then what the fuck...' The smell – that was not a day-old smell. That was the stench of decay, of rotting flesh, of the charnel house. What had they stumbled on? Some kind of dungeon? A Rillington Place, a Cromwell Street? He felt around for a light switch; the walls felt damp, sticky.

'Jesus!' He pulled his fingers back. 'Constable, give me a torch.'

'Sir.'

The dim beam barely crossed the large, darkened room; behind the green velvet drapes steel shutters barred the daylight. Bloated flies buzzed furiously in the fitful yellow beam, angry at being woken from their post-prandial sleep.

'What happened here?' Mike muttered to himself. 'What in hell's name...'

'Sir.' Terry's voice, trembling, beside him. 'Over there.' One shaky hand pointed to the far corner of the room, where something pale was moving slowly to and fro, to and fro. Mike aimed the beam of the torch.

It must have been roped at the heels and suspended, maybe from a beam in the ceiling; the body hung upside down, the head about four feet from the floor, everything from the neck to the tips of the hair concealed by a viscous black veil of blood that had gushed from a wide gash in the throat, congealing over the face, blocking the nostrils, holding the eyes open, the eyeballs covered with scabbing gore.

Mike's heart pounded in his chest – but he was the superior officer here. A Detective Inspector. It was for him to make a rational assessment, to execute a plan. It was for this that he was trained.

'Is that him?'

'Couldn't say for sure, sir,' said the sergeant. 'But... it looks about right. What's left of it.'

With a creak of the rope the body revolved slowly, revealing its back. The skin was hanging in a ragged flap from the shoulder blades, exposing bloody ribs. The rest of the thorax was empty.

'Call for reinforcements, sergeant.' The sergeant blinked stupidly, shock already robbing him of reason. 'Now!' Mike screamed in his face, and pushed him out of the room. He forced himself to look back at the dangling thing – the gently rotating, empty carcass. Oh sweet Jesus, Mike said to himself, where has it all gone? Where are the intestines? Where is the liver? The lungs?

A creak from the other side of the room – behind the sofa – Mike spun on his heels, almost skidding on something slippery underfoot. A kidney, perhaps? A scrap of spleen?

'Who's there?'

Low laughter, broken and wet sounding, like a man chewing a mouthful of chocolate pudding. Mike's eyes, adjusting to the low light, spotted the giblets hanging in rank festoons from the light fittings like party decorations in hell. A head appeared first, rising from behind the sofa, hair dark with blood, face a red mask from which crazy white eyes stood out like dinner plates, the irises pale to invisibility. The nose, covered in clots of gore like a hyaena's muzzle... And at last the mouth. But the mouth was obscured by the hands, and the hands were full, and hanging from them, glistening in the yellow torchlight, was something big and wet, the size of a newborn baby, ragged with bite marks.

The liver.

***

Light far away – a round white disk of light in still space – perfect and calm and still, as still as the moon, cold and clear and infinitely pure. And then the first spark of heat as life returns – is created? – and with life comes sensation and questions and memory and the endless daily search for the self that it born with waking and dies with sleeping.

Where am I? Who am I? The fear that, if those questions are not answered in the first two seconds, they may never be answered.

- Who are you? Who are you?

Voice outside my head eclipsing the moon, a black shadow of a voice against the pure white disk, darkness spoiling the pure cold light, making it hotter, closer, a bright glaring light shining in my eyes.

- Who are you?

Again, who am I? My eyes hurt, a deep pain, the pain of seeing.

I am... me, I say, but the voice is not yet outside me, not yet born.

- I am me. Outside me this time, older and weaker than I remember it, the voice of an old man coming from inside.

- And this. This is your story.

My story? What story?

- You expect us to believe it?

- It's the truth, I say. That's all that matters.

- The truth?

A shape moves across the light – a man's head, a blank mask, haloed by light.

- Yes. What I've told you is the truth.

Laughter – more than one voice.

- You think we'll buy that?

- I want to see my lawyer.

More laughter. I struggle to look around me, but my head is fixed, all I can see is the dark haloed head and around it, a fuzzy grey. Nothingness. Voices – the voices of the others.

- You don't get to see a lawyer here.

- Are you the police?

Laughter ripples round the room, from left to right, behind me, around again, I am surrounded.

- We are not the police, oh no. We are interested in your story. We have to talk about your story.

- It is the truth, I say again, but the words are stuck in my mouth like balls of cotton wool.

- I don't think you can be trusted, says the voice. You are... unreliable. You have lied about your identity.

- But everything I have said has been clear and simple and true.

True ... true ... true ... the word circles me in derisive echoes that descend into gibbers and squeals, meaningless noises, clackings of tongues and smacking of lips.

- We don't buy it.

Panic flutters inside me like a captive thing. What have I done? Where have I been taken?

- I've been framed, I scream. I've been framed.

- Framed, spits the voice. There are no framing devices here. Time moves forward, tick tock tick tock, one minute to the next, one hour, one day, one week. No flashbacks, no glimpses into the future, just second to second, minute to minute. See?

A clock appears before my face like a clock in a cartoon, a grinning face behind the hands – hands that are spinning insanely fast, backwards, their speed leaving lines in the air behind them.

- See? Nothing funny about that.

Laughter again, abruptly stopped. The clock explodes, cartoon cogs and springs flying into the grey. The dark haloed head returns.

- We don't *do* comedy. Nobody's laughing at your little jokes.

- I just wanted to ... entertain.

- Entertain! Granted, you can entertain. But is that enough? Can you make us emotionally identify with your characters?

The light behind the head has faded to a sun setting through an office window, no longer a demon's halo, just the dirty London sun going down behind offices and tower blocks and railway lines.

- I think so. I tried to make them sympathetic. I tried to introduce an element of romance.

- Granted, you can do romance. But romance is not enough. These days, we need sex. Can you do sex?

- I tried to. I made the story as sexually explicit as I could, within certain limits.

Muttering around me – I am seated at a table, with men and women in a circle – ordinary men and women, young and casually dressed.

- Granted, says the dark voice, now just a man in a suit with the sun setting behind him, illuminating his artfully scruffy hair. Granted, you can do sex. But anyone can do sex.

Any teenager with a mobile phone. Sex is not enough. You need suspense.

- I tried to create suspense. I gave you a crime, and launched an investigation.

- Granted, granted, the suspense was there, but nobody's buying crime any more. What people want is horror. Sheer, visceral horror.

The eyes around the table stare at me, a deep hunger behind them, lips pulling back over teeth that are too sharp, too many...

- I tried to give you horror. I overcame my own moral objections and described in revolting detail the cruelty that one human being can inflict on another, in a way that I thought would satisfy the most depraved appetite.

- Granted, the horror scenes were shocking. But shock is not enough.

Not enough, not enough, not enough chatter the voices round the table, as the sun grows larger and brighter, the room fades back to grey, and that devil's head is haloed once more by cold, deadly light.

- Then what? I've given you everything you could possibly want.

- But the thing is... The head is receding now, a black blob against the cold fire of the sun, the light bigger and brighter than ever, dazzling me so that I can no longer tell if I am seeing, or if I am blind... The thing is, well, you've entertained us, you've emotionally engaged us, you've given us sex and suspense and horror...

- Yes?

- But you're gay, aren't you?

- Gay?

- You're gay. Your writing is gay. Your books are gay. The marketing people say no, the buyers say no, the publicity people say no, the distributors say no, the newspapers and magazines and blogs and radio shows and TV shows say no, the book groups say no, the readers say no, the printers say no.

White out. Blind.

- No you see, no, we say no. No. No.

The Corrective Tender

Nick Campbell

They operated, on one level at least, out of a large, nondescript hotel in East Croydon, one new pale tower among many. I stood outside, feeling earthly and alone and full of cold. The wind was vicious now that the snow had settled, and as my last tissue disintegrated in an onslaught of hot, tropical-hued mucus, I suddenly wanted your handkerchief.

Shit! The years I pulled a face each time you shook that thing from your sleeve, grey and brown and covered in you presumably. Now you had me missing that too, and wondering who was pulling faces at it now. It was resilient, I thought. It had outstayed me.

My disembarkation was due that night. I'd arranged to meet my friend Bobbie for dinner, to make it feel like a proper holiday. I wanted to feel careless, free to be unlike me and behave unpredictably. I felt very me, standing outside the *Olympus*, watching the amber lights of traffic cross the overpass. We'd said six but I was late: which was fine, I told myself, just more guarantee she'd be there – very me, you'd say.

I decided I would have to wait for her in the restaurant lounge. I hadn't wanted to tackle those hotel corridors alone;

up here and down there just to reach Reception, Fire Exit signs both ends of the hall. On my arrival I'd been nervous, and gabbled about this at length to the fair young man behind the desk, who nodded, as if ready to take one end of his desk and move it for me himself, then arched an eyebrow and said, 'It'll just have to do for the duration of your stay, Mr Wright.'

It was a relief to see Bobbie, with that storm cloud of hair over her ever-watchful eyes, hovering by the buffet, and to see that she too looked unsettled by the place. When she saw me, her eyebrows shot up. 'You,' she mouthed, pointing, 'are not my friend.'

So she was still pleased to see me. When she was angry, she'd just blank me.

'You haven't taken your coat off,' I said.

'I thought I should wait,' she replied. 'You said they wouldn't let plebs in.'

'Evidently they do,' I said. 'Let's get a table.'

'I hate dining alone,' she complained.

'Well, what am I, Scotch mist?'

'Oh, I'm a dry white wine, thanks,' she said, watching me as I drew out her chair. 'And?'

I conceded an apology.

'That's a bit late too,' she said, smiling at last. 'They don't like me in here, you know,' she added, offhand.

I laughed. 'Who?'

'These funny boys running the place,' she said seriously. 'With their nice blonde hair and their eyes like oysters.'

'Oh,' I said.

One of them was at her elbow, ready for the drinks order. 'You should have a red wine,' she told me. 'For this virus. Not used to looking after yourself, are you?'

'Anyone can catch a cold,' I said, rather petulantly. I was thinking how hard it had been, since you left, to distinguish one feeling of burning eyes from another.

You might remember Bobbie: she'd have been out at New Year, over for birthdays. I never remember her saying much at parties, but we never really know how our friends behave when we're not there. You might have found her a match for you. We were first paired up in a school Physics experiment, tying batteries to wedges of cork, trying to make them float. I don't remember why. We were both drenched in five minutes. When the bell went I was laughing so hard I had a headache.

It isn't much to base love on, and so many years of shared history. Looking back I see several points we might have left each other and didn't. If we didn't see each other we were in contact. She was my confidante. She heard it all, often making interventions at a volume you wouldn't have expected. She may well have argued for you, in fact.

'Now Liam,' she said, menus put away, 'What are they doing to you, again?'

She'd had her share of good grace now, I thought. 'They don't do anything *to* me.'

'So it's *not* a sex change,' she said.

I'd memorised a couple of lines off the website. 'It's more a *life transplant*.'

She pulled a face. 'Sounds a bit godly. You've not joined a cult, Liam? Without me? How much have you paid them?' When I stumbled in replying, her eyes widened. 'That was a joke! What's this – this life transplant thing, costing?'

'Only about as much as a holiday. Well, a quite expensive holiday.'

She was swigging her wine anxiously. 'In Croydon? I got here on the train, £10 return!'

'Oh,' I said enigmatically, 'I'm going a lot further than Croydon.'

'Ooh, impressed.'

'Anyway, it's not like *paying*,' I said. A person's disapproval can be quite rallying. 'It's more a donation. The Tender are only a small consortium, you see, with big plans.'

'For you?' she said, with a giggle.

'For everything.' I had finished my drink already. One of the soft-eyed young men refilled my glass before I'd asked; I stopped him and ordered a bottle. This wasn't quite the fun night out I'd wanted. I noticed he barely looked at Bobbie.

'One of your lot,' she said.

'Not sure,' I replied.

'And they all –' She leaned across and lowered her voice, quite conspicuously in the rather quiet restaurant lounge. 'They all look exactly the—'

'Similar,' I said, wishing she hadn't noticed. It was hard explaining things here, not knowing who was who. The longer it took, the drunker we became. 'The whole hotel's part of it. Tonight they send me off.'

'Lovely,' she said. 'Off where?'

'Well, this hotel,' I said, 'but in another world, parallel.'

'A parallel world...?' Bobbie looked nonplussed. I tried to explain.

'Each decision we make in this world causes another one to split off, one that might have been...'

'Oh, I know all that stuff,' she said with a gesture. 'But where do you come in?'

'It's the Tender's programme. To make these little amendments throughout the worlds. Righting wrongs. Balancing out the universes one at a time.'

Our food arrived.

'But what's so wrong about this world?'

'Isn't it obvious?' I smiled. 'It's Joseph!'

Silence. I ate, still smiling, oblivious, till I looked her in the eye and saw how sad she looked. 'A world where he loves me – where we belong together. Now do you see what this has all been for?'

More silence. I tried changing the subject. She, though, was keen to get back to my escapade and how set against it she was. We fell into an argument like an old song we both knew. We'd had enough set-to's in our time, in bedrooms and on street corners, about one or another's lapse in judgement, going back to old loves being a bit of a theme (though never quite like this). What Bobbie must not have known is that generally when she thought I was going astray, I agreed but couldn't say.

Not this time. The thought of seeing you – or someone just like you – again, so soon, made me impervious to her argument. It was good to argue, in fact, to get all this stuff out in the open – because I had sat on my bed in the hotel room thinking this through for an hour before I met her, and I had never been so sure of a decision. Just saying your name had made me feel so good.

'So, *It's A Wonderful Life*,' she said at last, worn down and pissed off about it. 'A world without Liam.'

'No,' I said, 'they wouldn't let me have that. Too confusing I suppose.'

'But what do you do about your double? Shove him under a bus?'

'He'll be moving on too,' I said. 'Tomorrow there'll be another me here. A new me.' Picking up my phone and my house-keys from the suitcase in the wardrobe. Ringing her to say let's go out and drink in the delights of East Croydon. No chocolate on her Cappuccino.

'Can you be sure?' she said.

'It's what I'll do,' I told her. 'And we'll wander the city centre with our hangovers, checking it's not that world where Rome never fell.'

And she laughed. So we parted on good terms, or near enough. Although, at the time, we didn't know we had parted at all.

I couldn't sleep. Too much drink, and I was waiting for the signal, for the phone to ring twice, a soft knock on the door. Instead, at one o'clock I saw a white mist creep under the door. Nothing more than that – if I wanted to get anywhere, I'd have to venture out. I dressed as instructed: numbered watch-strap, black trunks, white cotton robe. The hallway was heaped with steamy clouds like dirty washing. I'd not noticed before how the wallpaper peeled away where it met the skirting boards, but at last I realised why none of the communal areas were carpeted. I thought it would sting as I walked into it but it was oddly cool, like something from a smoke machine.

The actual baths, though, were in the basement, and a classier affair, though not without their faux-rock cave effect and rose-coloured lighting. So I was to wait here.

You'll know, I'd never visited a steam baths before, but I breathed in deep, longing for the swirling clouds to penetrate and split the thick weight pressing on my tear ducts. It smelled unexpectedly bitter. Though it might have been just the state of the plumbing, I told myself it was some exotic herb, transported from a snowy mountain to ready the minds of we travellers betwixt dimensions. This might be a tantric, psychical voyage after all. I had wondered whether the Tender themselves, with their calm demeanour and their watchmaker fascination with the checks and balances of the universe, didn't hail from some secluded village in Switzerland.

There was no machine noise. Nothing seemed immediately in the offing. Where and how might it happen? There were deeper rooms to explore, farther pools, glass doors swinging shut with a whisper. Other clients wandered languidly between them, faceless in the mists as shadows. I had an urge to speak with one of them, ask a question, make small talk. But a heady silence hung over the room that I knew it would be terrible to break. The silhouettes of those other men – going where? coming from where? – were uncannily like reflections in a hall of mirrors, and the thought made me shudder.

I cast aside my robe and slid into a pool so hot I felt as if I was falling away from myself, like pages off a book dropped in the bath. Time crept by, and every adjustment I made was torture. S

I suddenly felt alone – gratefully alone, because the whole trip seemed such a folly. And then I felt a hand take mine, and help me from the pool.

It was one of the Corrective agents. He examined my watch-strap, nodded smartly, led me away, his fingers cool around my wrist. As we marched, my heart beat and my mind whirled; I almost skidded off the poolside's wet tiling into a bathful of hot water and young men. Instead we continued, through dizzying circles of rooms of steam and smoke, on and down, on and down. When he left me, I was woozy, eyes smarting. But the weight of those pungent fumes were no longer about me.

I found myself in a corridor on the ground floor, near the kitchens. The lights were off in there and the door was locked. I waited and began to shiver and then I sneezed, twice, hard. Nothing more seemed to be happening.

Retreating to my bed, I fell asleep in a spirit of blind trust.

At six I woke myself with a wild coughing fit which left me more awake than I usually am at midday. I lay in the ringing silence and thought of the night's unsatisfying end.

How typical that it should fail with me, the world's worst complainer. I wondered whether I even wanted a second try, remembering with what clarity I had seen myself, as I stewed beneath the pavements of Croydon. I might manage a full refund. I could slip away and forget all about it.

So long as it *had* been a failure.

I perused my hotel room. I was certain that sheeny pink satin of the bedspread, the oak-effect bedside cabinet, the green baize pinboard scorched by a lamp, were all unchanged, though it was hard to check a memory of something you had never noticed. The man on the front desk was the same as the day before, too. He was adamant, though: the transaction had been made satisfactorily.

'I'm supposed to give you this when you check out later,' he said, passing me a translucent plastic folder full of documents, 'but you read this over breakfast, Mr Wright. That's all our legal material. If you're not satisfied with our treatment, the Tender is unstinting in its restitutionary acts. But you'd be our first, Mr Wright.' His eyes twinkled, and I went obediently to breakfast, clutching my folder.

I examined the bacon machine, the meagre light outside. I turned the pages of a newspaper, my heart crashing in my chest. They'd reassured me the new world would be indistinguishable from the old, but surely some quirk must give it away?

I showered. Had he – the prior me – stood here yesterday, and did he wash the back of his neck first, by instinct, as I did? Had we both had our hair cut that Tuesday before, by the same chatty woman from Hungary who didn't like Abba (everybody likes Abba, surely she could not be repeated in every universe throughout eternity) – and where was he going anyway, with the Tender?

I collected my suitcase. I checked out, still before eight. I caught myself examining the pattern on a pigeon's back and burst into tears. There was just one way to gauge this new reality.

It felt too early to phone Bobbie, so I hurried to the station, swathed in commuters with serious expressions. My secret burned in me so hotly, as we huddled together in the carriage, I thought it would be obvious I was the new guy in town. At Redhill I fumbled with the door control, as if it was as fiddly as those latches on the Paris metro. The world had never felt more unfamiliar.

Your practice, I know, is on Smith Street, and so it was here too, though I couldn't tell if it looked any different – we never visited each other's work. But you were always talking about Petra, and as soon as this woman at reception turned round, I knew it was her, and trying to remain calm, explained that I was a friend of Doctor Steadman's and could she let him know I was waiting – would and could wait, however long he needed, thank you.

Taking my seat I remembered my phone, tucked away in my suitcase: you might have the same number, and I could have just called that. Was that better? Presumptuous? I left it where it was, and sat, trembly, coughing and sneezing, amongst the other invalids, watching daytime telly. Longing for some giveaway detail, amongst the hairdo banter.

I saw a man standing the behind the counter and talking with Petra, and looking at me with deep suspicion. He must have been somewhere in his late forties, a tall man with hair, eyes and eyebrows so dark that his thoughts were as legible as a cartoon. As he caught my eye he turned his head in a questioning but familiar expression, and I realised it was this world's Joseph. Exactly like you.

I meant to smile but I couldn't. I rose and met him at the counter's swing door, and we went into out into early morning air, still quiet, frost on the path still undemolished.

'Forgotten something?' he said, jutting his jaw.

It occurred me for the first time that another me had ended things for us, the same few weeks ago that you had. Justifiably, he was confused. He loomed over me and shifted his weight uncertainly in a way I don't remember ever seeing you do. It felt as if he would fall on me if I made a false move. I took a deep breath, choosing my words, and the cold air sliced at my throat as if ulterior to it, producing more lunatic coughing.

'I've changed my mind,' I said, wiping my eyes.

'Hmm,' he said. 'Here.' He proffered his handkerchief.

I thought we might meet a few times over the following weeks, defining our territory. But when I invited him round the week after, he arrived laden with citrus fruits and eucalyptus oils, and before we discussed anything important, he had me lying on my stomach on the kitchen table, he was pulling up my shirt and smacking my back just below the shoulder blades to loosen the weight in my chest, and then I was inhaling steam from a bowl of freshly boiled water. We ate chocolate ginger together, and he lectured me.

And I only didn't kiss him that night because of not infecting him. What if my virus had never existed on this world, and I killed him off with love?

I thought these sorts of thoughts when I woke in the middle of the night coughing, but a fortnight after, I was well again and it was starting to look a lot like spring.

We went to Homebase and sifted ideas for the garden he shared with his neighbour. In that last year of us together, we'd done nothing like that, because whatever I picked up, seed or shrub or implement or ornament, made you screw up your face: 'For God's sake,' you said once, in a low tone, 'I'm not actually your Grandmother, you know.' But Joseph suspected me of having a good eye for colour, and perhaps I was asking him more questions than I did you. I suppose was being more careful now. We were beginning anew, not quite from scratch but a position of mutual confusion. We hadn't discussed 'where we went wrong', hadn't negotiated a thing.

It was a while before I unpacked the suitcase from the *Olympus*, not having needed my phone. I had missed calls and a five minute voicemail from my first day here, which I deleted without listening to. I went to the Corrective Tender's website ('Ever Feel You're Living in the Wrong World? Been Hurt In a Grievance Which Isn't Your Fault?') and added my glowing testimony to the others there. I took care to delete my History afterward; for good measure, I went through my inbox with a fine-tooth comb as well.

I chose not to explain the circumstances of my return. You and he must essentially be composed of the same stuff, after all, and capable of all the same behaviour. If he even once tried to see me as you had done, wouldn't he have spotted all the same flaws you did? His love was like yours in your first flush, but it was surely still contingent on my behaviour – it couldn't be a constant. That would be worrying.

I'd been signed off work, but was back in time for summer exams. At a barbeque to celebrate end of term, I brought Joseph along for the first time and proudly showed him off. I don't know that you would have come – he and you must both have had to take leave – but he was often more pliant than you, I found. I suppose I would be just the same for you.

And in the two and a half years we'd been together, I'd never felt so part of something mutual and healthy. We wrapped ourselves in one another, and didn't see friends so often. The only notice I had of this was in a birthday card from Bobbie, which ended: 'Ignore me if you will, Mr Wright, but I will see you again soon, my dear.' I wasn't ignoring her, of course – she was at the back of my mind again, that's just how things went.

I did wonder sometimes how much the Bobbie of this world knew. Had she been in East Croydon that night in early February, with the prior me? I couldn't help but look on the pair of them as conspirators and secret-keepers. Better to spend time with Mum and Dad, who saw no change in me, and who had never really known Joseph, and found they loved him, his sweetness and wit. They shared a passion for Tchaikovsky and would sometimes meet to see performances when I was out of town.

I did go away more often. I was learning I was not the man I had been. Happiness or peace of mind or something other had made me more assertive, more restless. It wasn't always easy doing the same old with Joseph. When I tried, for example, to be clever, to use what insight I'd gained from that last month with you, when I tried to change my ways to meet the criticisms you had, then I saw his first real deviations from you. I never cooked for you, you'd complained: I tried cooking for Joseph, and he begged me to stop. I'd become too staid for you, couldn't act as young as I looked; now I tried acting impulsively, talked about going out – or texted, late, to change plans. Joseph reacted coolly to much of this, and sometimes, to my extreme chagrin, even looked bored by it. At last he told me, in no uncertain terms, that I wasn't behaving like myself and he didn't like it.

The problem reoccurred in bed, and worse. The first time we slept together, we both just went for it, the only distraction being that I kept trying to check him for discrepancies by the light from the landing, hair in the wrong place, a different smell. He didn't seem to mind, and everything tallied. Other times, though, I found myself working like a trendy chef, always trying to mix things up, trying to find the thing he liked that you didn't, or things you never knew you liked. I thought there must be something more I could be doing

He huffed in frustration as I worked away with all the wrong moves. Then he laughed and kissed me, and made me lie down where I always used to lie, and we did it just the way you always liked it, and he came.

I was thrown, but learnt my lesson. I stuck to the script and it was more or less bliss, but better with a run out now and then. My flat looked so unhomely anyway – in that world and this, we had sold so many of our possessions to meet the requirements of the Tender, and it reminded me unpleasantly of that secret jumping of the tracks. Then one day in early December I came home and my neighbours gave me a present. A young girl had left it, they said; they'd had to explain I was often away, because she looked about ready to wait all day for me. I didn't open the parcel. I was in the habit now of binning any postcards or letters that arrived with Bobbie's hand on the envelope.

Next morning I woke to find we were in both a new world. The same world, transformed: Joseph and I, peacefully entwined. I thought helplessly of the Tender, and imagined the point where this reality noiselessly diverged from the one of the night before: was that how it worked? Or were worlds quieting under the Tender's coaxing, their checks and balances? Were they healing over as the corrections totalled up? Outside the sky was lowering again.

The dark haired weight of Joseph's arm was over my face, almost suffocating. I extricated myself and kissed his eyes.

'I think it's time to move house,' I said. 'Us both, together, I mean.'

He was pleased, almost childishly. You always liked your own space, exactly where you did, but he was ready to go wherever I suggested, which was out of London altogether. I didn't like to feel so haunted by my past, I told him.

It was the wrong time to year to move but all the same we started looking, Googling up wonderful and terrible images to tease each other with. I found myself preferring hopelessly fantastical solutions. Isolated farmhouses where the nearest neighbours were miles away. Nowhere for either of us to work, but somehow I wanted to roll us both up in each other, lock and bar the door.

He laughed at the idea and kissed me.

As if in tribute to that mad idea, or in practice for the future, he agreed to go away for New Year's, renting a hotel room where nobody knew us. I'd always wanted to see winter in Brighton, and it obliged that evening, snow falling and falling on a jagged sea the colour of those glass chippings you see on graves. We had lobster in a fish restaurant almost on the seafront, and slightly drunkenly Joseph began talking about our breakup, things I'd said. I pretended I wasn't listening and he looked hurt, but we managed not to have an argument on our special night out

We went back to the hotel and had a few drinks in the bar. They had a DJ, pink and white balloons. It started up again: why did you leave? Why did you change your mind? Had you met someone else?

I'd not noticed how wound up Joseph had got. Now and then he turned on a smile and I saw with some horror what a blind this was, and how often he'd used it. I tried to make something up, but it was difficult to sound convincing on the spot, slightly pissed, slightly scared. He put a hand on my shoulder and told me I needed to calm down. 'I've watched you, these last months,' he said, 'Worrying we'll run into somebody you don't want me to know about. But you've got me to yourself here.'

He kissed my hand in what felt a suddenly embarrassing gesture, and I told him so. He laughed at himself, or forced himself to, for my sake or for auld lang's syne, which an offensively happy table of people had begun to sing one hour early.

I was worked up too, over-alert, reading other people's conversations. I had a way of calming myself. I'd look again for that sign that this was not my world. Labels on bottles, words to the Macy Gray song the DJ was playing. God, me and Bobbie used to duet to that all night, but what were the words? A meteorite strike would be more easily distinguished.

I counted the buttons on Joseph's shirt and apologised, but he was too reasonable. I wondered how the prior me ever broke away from him. 'Let's go,' I said. 'Somewhere a bit, you know, gayer. Explore the town. Maybe meet someone...'

Joseph tilted his head as if considering. He and I hadn't talked about it, so far as I knew (after all, I'd begun to think, the way things were, why shouldn't our relationship have been different to his, all the way down? – not a subtle distinction but a whole other branch in the surface pattern of the universe) but taking someone home was a recurring topic with us. I'd never said how much I knew you'd like it, and you'd never pushed it enough for me to decline. But here – New Year's Eve – it felt an obvious suggestion.

'No,' Joseph said. 'We're not going out. But we are meeting someone. I had a call this morning from a friend of yours. She saw on your Facebook or somewhere that you were coming here and said we should meet. As a surprise!'

'I've left Facebook,' I said stonily.

'Or something,' he said weakly.

'She must have phoned my parents,' I said. I thought she might, eventually.

'Is it alright?' he said. 'She sounded fun, and she knew *you*. Was telling me all about your wasted youth and all sorts...'

'We can't,' I said, 'Not on New Year's Eve. I want it to be just us.'

The black mark of his eyebrows lowered, almost covering his eyes. 'You keep saying that,' he said, 'but you know it's not what you want. We're almost strangling one another.'

'What? What are you trying to say?' My voice was raised, but just because of the music, I thought. 'You picked the right place, didn't you?'

I wanted to storm out of the bar and out through the hotel lobby, down to the sea's edge and the space beyond the light, but we were pressed too tightly in with people. I couldn't move my arms to lift my drink to my lips, couldn't hardly breathe. She was making her way through the crowd to meet us, somewhere. Even before I saw her coming, in her party frock, I could feel her closing in, with a shy, knowing smile, wetting her lips to speak.

Contributors

Paul Magrs lives and writes in Manchester. He is the author of the Brenda and Effie Mysteries and the Iris Wildthyme novels, and various other books, too. His most recent novel is *666 Charing Cross Road*.

Stewart Sheargold lives in Sydney, Australia. He has written short stories and scripts for the Doctor Who, Bernice Summerfield and Gallifrey Big Finish ranges, and has contributed stories to Obverse collections, as well as an electronic collection of short stories for Manleigh books. He is, after four years, finally putting the finishing touches on two children's novels. He plans to write a third.

Gene Hult has had many books for children and young adults published under a pseudonym. He writes freelance full-time from his sunny apartment in the Manhattan neighborhood of Washington Heights, a few avenues away from where he was born. He lives there with his sweet and pesky kitten Bernard and his bitchy older cat Mabel, and he probably should get out of the apartment more often.

Matt Cresswell has taught Shakespeare to teenagers, but still loves literature. He left Leicester with a professionally useless degree in Creative Writing, and now lives in a dodgy part of Manchester. He is the editor of Glitterwolf Magazine, showcasing LGBT writers and artists. More of his short fiction can be found in his ebook collection *If You Weren't Real, I Would Make You Up*. www.mattcresswell.com

Bob Smith is author of the bestselling humorous memoirs *Openly Bob* (winner of a Lambda Literary Award) and *Way to Go, Smith* and the novel *Selfish and Perverse*, which was one of three finalists for the Edmund White Award for Debut Fiction. As a standup comic, he broke barriers as the first openly gay comedian to appear on *The Tonight Show* and was featured in his own HBO comedy special. His comic essays and articles have appeared in *The Advocate* and *Out*. He grew up in Buffalo, New York, and lives in New York City.

Cody Quijano-Schell is an author and graphic designer from Iowa, USA. He grew up watching *Bewitched's* Darrin Stevens on TV and decided commercial art would be something fun to do as an adult. Tony Nelson made being an astronaut seem exciting too. He reckons working for Obverse Books sort of combines the two professions.

Jonathan Kemp was born in Manchester and lives in London. His first novel, London Triptych, won the Authors' Club Best First Novel Award. A collection of prose poems, *Twentysix*, was published in 2011, and his second novel, *Hannah Rose*, is forthcoming in 2012 (all published by Myriad Editions). He teaches creative writing and comparative literature at Birkbeck.

Joseph Lidster has written scripts for radio and television, including episodes of *Torchwood* and *The Sarah Jane Adventures*. He is currently working on scripts for other TV projects as well as a micro-budget film. You can follow him on twitter at twitter.com/joelidster.

Wayne Clews was born in Congleton, Cheshire. He studied in Lancaster and Manchester and since then has worked at various theatres and bookshops and as a freelance journalist. His short fiction has appeared in Comma, City Secrets and Blank Media. He currently lives in Salford with his partner Iain, where he is working on a novel.

Scott Handcock lives in Cardiff where he works for the BBC Drama department at BBC Wales (including stints on *The*

Sarah Jane Adventures and *Doctor Who*). As a freelancer, he has contributed several scripts for BBC Audio and Big Finish Productions, and is currently acting as producer and director on a number of their upcoming ranges.

Rupert Smith is the author of several novels, including the Stonewall Award-winning *Man's World*. He has written genre fiction of various types under various names, notably erotica as James Lear (including the best-selling The Back Passage) and blockbusting 'women's fiction' as Rupert James. For over twenty years he was a journalist, contributing to dailies, weeklies and monthlies; for eight years he was TV critic for The Guardian. He lives in London.

Nick Campbell is an administrator and research student living in London. He blogs about books at leaf-pile.blogspot.co.uk, and in 2010 and 2011 was a judge of the Green Carnation Prize for great modern gay writing.